Praise for *The Stars Are Not Yet Bells*

"This poignant novel is a testament to love and loss [and] the sacrifices made for love."

—*The Washington Post*

"A prophetic fever dream sprung from a singular imagination. Hannah Lillith Assadi is an incomparable stylist and a fearless storyteller. This novel is a lush, addicting, daring wonder."

—Claire Vaye Watkins, author of *I Love You but I've Chosen Darkness*

"The beauty of Assadi's prose and the splendid depiction of a love that transcends death make for a singular rendition of an oft-told story. This will leave readers undone."

—*Publishers Weekly* (starred review)

"A lyrical, beautiful writer . . . the musicality of her language carries the emotion of it in such a way that's unique to her."

—Shelly Oria, *Los Angeles Review of Books* podcast

"A poetically stunning and heartfelt story of love, loss, and loneliness . . . Assadi wonderfully keeps both Elle and the reader on the same pace toward discovery, remembrance, and closure. . . . It was the beauty of Assadi's writing that never failed to astonish me, encapsulated in elegant prose with lyrical, resonant language, chock-full of rich descriptions with haunting imagery and sensory detail."

—*The Michigan Daily*

"The poetic beauty of the writing and a certain swirling gothic passion and drama bowl the reader along. . . . An unusual, intense, experimental novel."
—*Daily Mail* (London)

"A heartbreaking and profoundly visionary book. Hannah Assadi movingly renders the kaleidoscopic nature of memory—revealing not only one woman's disordered heart and mind, but the way our consciousness recombines shards of memory to create a glittering, prismatic view of a life. I wanted to stay in Assadi's shimmering sentences for as long as I could."
—Emily Fridlund, author of *History of Wolves*

"A haunting elegy for loss, desire, and memory."
—*Kirkus Reviews*

"A luminous and deeply moving portrait of the end of life and the persistence of desire. While Hannah Lillith Assadi's characters are forced to deny the truth of themselves and who they love, in her assured hands the extraordinary beauty of life and love and the natural world is never lost."
—JoAnne Tompkins, author of *What Comes After*

"A rich, mesmerizing novel, in which waves of overlapping memory erode the landscape of a woman's life until only feeling remains—both in the story and in the reader."
—Simon Van Booy, author of *The Illusion of Separateness*

THE STARS ARE NOT YET BELLS

Also by Hannah Lillith Assadi

Sonora

THE STARS ARE NOT YET BELLS

Hannah Lillith Assadi

RIVERHEAD BOOKS * *New York*

RIVERHEAD BOOKS

An imprint of Penguin Random House LLC
penguinrandomhouse.com

The Library of Congress has catalogued the Riverhead hardcover edition as follows:
Names: Assadi, Hannah Lillith, author.
Title: The stars are not yet bells / Hannah Lillith Assadi.
Description: First edition. | New York: Riverhead Books, 2022.
Identifiers: LCCN 2020051357 (print) | LCCN 2020051358 (ebook) |
ISBN 9780593084366 (hardcover) | ISBN 9780593084465 (ebook)
Classification: LCC PS3601.S74 S73 2022 (print) | LCC PS3601.S74 (ebook)
DDC 813/.6—dc23
LC record available at https://lccn.loc.gov/2020051357
LC ebook record available at https://lccn.loc.gov/2020051358

First Riverhead hardcover edition: January 2022
First Riverhead trade paperback edition: January 2023
Riverhead trade paperback ISBN: 9780593084472

Printed in the United States of America
1st Printing

Book design by Cassandra Garruzzo

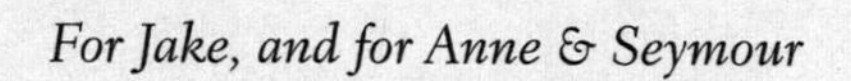

For Jake, and for Anne & Seymour

The earth is not yet a garden
about to be turned. The stars
are not yet bells that ring
at night for the lost.
It is much too late.

"My Mother on an Evening in Late Summer," Mark Strand

PART I

Spring

I.

It is not yet the end. Moss descends from the oaks, thick as curtains, veiling the night's secrets from the living. A wild mare and her foal are out to feed before the dawn. Seagulls bark their hunger at the sky. And Lyra, our island, remains above the sea. The ocean has not engulfed all this, even though I have woken from that dream I've had again and again over the decades. In last night's rendering, after the island had burned and sunken into the waters and all the stars had fallen into the Atlantic, I could still swim. And beneath the surface, wandering among the blue constellations like a mermaid, at last I found Gabriel.

2.

But it is not the story of a drowned ghost haunting my dreams that Dr. Madera wants from me. He says I must focus on the facts. Dr. Madera has commanded that I report the story of myself, *the real story*, every morning. Should I get lost, he has offered me helpful mnemonic exercises: *What is your age? What is your name? Where do you live? What year is it? Who is your husband? What are the names of your children? What is the weather like today?*

The wind smells of rain. My name is Elle Ranier. It is May the thirteenth, 1997. A voice talks at me from the radio, telling me that the market has turned for the worse, the Israelis and Palestinians are at war, snow falls late in the north. The broadcast makes it sound as if the world is finally ending. I no longer tremble at signs of the apocalypse, since my own was prophesized for me in a fluorescent medical office some time ago.

At the start of the Second World War, I moved from New York City to Lyra Island, population four hundred—most of whom, until these last years, were employed by my husband, Simon. We have lived since then on this strip of sand, woolly with oak, off the coast of southern Georgia. The dunes here shimmer, white as snow. Wild horses roam, ancient and unapproachable as unicorns. Storms trample us in this part of the world; we are the midwife of the ocean's wrath. Hurricanes have ravaged my garden many times over. Until this year I have always been able to revive my rosebushes. Our home was built on the foundation of a previous one, which was built on the foundation of one before that; both houses burned to the ground a century apart. The island has never wanted us.

Back in '41, the three of us—Gabriel, Simon, and I—had anchored at the dock on the river's side, rather than the ocean's, where the irreverent tangle of oak recalls the woods of some fairy tale. I knew even then that I'd become lost in them. The path to the house was scarcely marked by an ancient sandy trail; there has only ever been the one dirt road carving its way through the island, from the town in the south to the northern settlement. Our house stood on Lyra's highest ground, right in the middle. It was Elijah, at first the groundskeeper and later Simon's ship watch leader, who guided us to our new habitat, which stank of earth and ocean and fire. We were city people and startled by the sound of our own feet crushing the leaves beneath us, but it was not the land itself that would curtail our welcome.

Once the house was before us, I gazed at it in awe, the stone stairways rising into a menagerie of vines veiling more windows than I could count, the grounds so spacious that a wild horse gnawing on the lawn seemed the size of a dog. Even the light overhead was of a different quality, more persistent in its splendor. I wondered to myself how a person would not go missing in such a place.

After some moments engaged in this reverie, I noticed that Gabriel had indeed vanished. I turned to Elijah, mustering what composure I could, and asked after his whereabouts.

"Mr. Simon says your cousin's to be staying in the old shed," Elijah responded. "So I pointed him on his way."

"They've done it up for him quite nicely, Elle," Simon said. "And wait until you see the bridal quarters."

I had not yet had a chance to visit even the bathroom when Mr. Clarke Senior, the mayor, materialized from the ghostly spread of oak with a rifle in hand. "Well then, Ranier, you've found our Lyra," he said by way of greeting.

Back then, the island still answered to the Clarkes, as it had since the beginning of American time—that is, after Lyra was stolen by the Clarkes from its indigenous, most of whom had been driven from the earth. The family had derived its fortune first from gold and then from steel, but they had fallen out of the financial favor they once held. It was from the Clarkes, I learned later, that Simon's father had purchased the land where our new house stood. Theirs, too, had stood there once.

It was not only Clarke we would meet that day, but an entire cadre of his loyal locals. One by one they emerged from the woods, armed at his side, as if our puny party represented the German invasion feared along the Atlantic coast. Whatever sudden inferiority they might have felt toward Simon, with regard to financial standing on the island, was upstaged by this display in military might. Simon's stature seemed to shrink, from its former six feet to something less, as he stepped behind Elijah and then very nearly behind me, his slender and helpless wife.

It was Gabriel who spoke at last, reemerging a wraith from Lyra's wild. He stood before the militia in the manner of an immortal, unarmed and grinning. "Who knew paradise was so easy to find?" he replied, on our behalf. And so ended the short-lived standoff.

Simon retired early that evening, claiming exhaustion, so Gabriel and I walked through the grounds toward the sea, which I had not yet seen. The island was more feral back then. Or perhaps it is only so in memory. Moss tickled our shoulders as we walked; above it the stars were bright as fireflies, a dream of the trees.

"Simon is still shaken up over that reception from Mr. Clarke this afternoon," I said. "He even said something about returning to New York. Wondered if he should write his father."

Gabriel shrugged. "Clarke was only trying to spook him, Elle. Show Mr. Simon he might be the boss right now, but not for long."

"So that's what their whole circus was about?" I asked.

"I was hiding in the woods listening in on 'em before they ever approached. They were goin' on about not letting any Yankee take what's here," Gabriel replied. "I heard one of 'em say it's *blue ground*, Elle. That there's diamonds in the water—or maybe some kind of jewels even prettier than diamonds. 'Course then another said that was all just an old slave story."

"There it is," I said, distracted as the trees parted. Before us suddenly were the iridescent dunes, and beyond them, that canvas of impassive, violet sea. Nothing would ever be so magnificent as that first glimpse.

"Yes, there she is," Gabriel said, drawing me into him. "My sham cousin, alone with me at last."

That was our first day on Lyra, a far more poetic day to die. Instead I've lived to hear Dr. Madera diagnose me with a disease that befalls the old, that destroys memory—my own, surely, but also the memory of the world as it once was.

I stare out the window and imagine all my most beautiful memories, stretching vast and deep as the ocean, shimmering blue as a mirage beyond the scrum of oak. I am losing the Atlantic, losing all that makes me Elle: my facts.

3.

The first fact that left me, as far as I can recall, was the existence of my keys. It wasn't as if I couldn't find them. One afternoon, suddenly, it was as though they'd never existed at all. It was scorching already, the rite of southern spring, and the mosquitoes had laid waste to my calves. As I stood there at my front door on my pockmarked legs, struggling with the doorknob, I thought someone was playing a cruel joke on me. I understood that the door was locked, but not how to undo the state of it being so. I felt like the dreamer whose mouth won't sound though she is screaming.

Finally, I thought to go around to the garden and call for Elijah. I was screaming for his assistance when Ethel appeared. I hardly recognized her—her hair was nearly all white.

"What are you goin' on about?" she asked. I explained to her that I could not get into the house, that the door was standing in my way.

"Where is Elijah?" I demanded again.

"*My* Elijah?" Ethel was frightened, as if I'd pointed to some specter in our midst. Then the fear passed and a curious expression formed on her face.

"Well, what's taking him so long?" I asked.

Ignoring me, she pulled a large chain of keys out from the pocket of her dress and walked me like her darling through the front door. "You forgetting things again?" she asked. "Go on and sell my soul to Satan if my own Elijah was resurrected for your eyes to behold before my own."

Outside I hear sirens. The oaks do not mind the interruption. Only we humans are given pause by the reminder of death. Perhaps everyone on the island is dying. It is happening to all of us, all at once, the planet over. The rain finally begins. The morning review of my facts disintegrates beneath the ambulance's wailing soundtrack. I hope there is a little room somewhere in the universe where all the lost bits have gone to hide. "Second star to the left and straight on till morning," I say aloud for nobody.

The wall calendar says it is Sunday, and on Sundays, for as long as we have lived here, Simon attends the Baptist church on the north end of the island. There he plays piano for the congregants, most of whom are or have been his employees. And on Saturday evenings, for as long as we have lived here, I have played for him the part of the church chorus as he rehearses the list of songs he plans to play the next morning. That is, until just days ago, when suddenly I could no longer stand the cacophony of what had always been melodious music to me. In fact, all I could hear in it were sirens. I screamed at Simon to *Stop, please—it's torture*. He stood and closed the fallboard with little ceremony, then kissed me on the forehead. "As you wish, Elle."

I rather wish he trembled with rage instead. But that has never been his way. It was never for me that Simon reserved his passion. Throughout his years of secret dalliances, there was only one I believe he loved, and that was the gentleman from Louisiana. We have never said anything about the lovers, nor about the geologist from New Orleans. I have always protected Simon, and he has always protected me. When I was young, I believed I was saving my life by marrying him. But one never knows how a life may be saved or destroyed until it is too late.

So we both had lovers who were originally from New Orleans. But unlike Simon's, my affair has primarily been with a dead man.

I have only the one photograph of Gabriel and me. There is so little proof he ever existed before or after that day. My body, in the photo, has turned blond from the summer. Our knees just barely touch, but I can still feel the hair on my thighs stand at the gesture. He hands me his cigarette and I can taste him on it. I have never before wanted anything so much. The smoke wanders in and out of me. And then I collapse, coughing.

As the camera shutter clicks, he whispers a secret in my ear. The cigarette remains in my hand; his mouth is pressed against my hair. Desire is hardly the word. There is nothing else, in that moment, for us. I don't remember where we were, who was taking the photograph, only that we'd just recently met. I was still a girl, barely seventeen. Time began its advance with Gabriel. Memories of the time before him belong to some other child's life.

Gabriel's punishment for me has been that he will always remain young, always the face in the photograph, while I've watched my body age. He is forever the man whose legs were entwined with mine that summer, who carried me out into the sea at Coney Island despite my shrieks that I couldn't swim, whose weight later pressed down on that body of mine, now long gone. It was beneath him that I first felt what it was to melt the edges of myself into another. I wonder if he had a sense then, in the picture, that he would die so young. I wonder what his secret was, stilled forever in my ear by the camera, that I will never hear again.

Like the sirens before, the shrill ring of the telephone shatters my daydream. There is so much more noise in the world now than there once was. Simon announces that no one on the island has died. A kitten climbed up a tree and the ambulance—Lyra has only the one—came to rescue it. "Thank God, right?" he says into the phone.

"So, we all aren't dying?" I ask him quite seriously.

"Would you like anything from town, darling?" Simon asks, ignoring me.

A time machine, I want to say. My own cat, Mina, stares at me curiously, as if I were engaged in a conversation with ghosts by using the telephone. I shoo her away but she returns to my side. Before I became sick, she never paid me any attention at all. The mice and the raccoons in the garden were far more interesting. Lately, though, I have become a subject of great curiosity to her. Ever since I realized that Mina will remember me longer than I her, I have an irrational resentment toward her. I hate that she will roam among my things, my purses and coats and blouses, free to destroy them once their occupant is gone. "Your friend is okay!" I shout at her, referring to the reckless kitten of Simon's phone call.

Beholding the cat, I suddenly ache from the simple fact of her pretty face. If life weren't full of so much beauty—the sweet mischief in Mina's gaze, wild horses running down the blue beaches of everywhere, a spell of spring rain, the lilac dawn and its twin in dusk, the silk of a first kiss, Gabriel's knee grazing mine, the stupidity and ephemerality and naïve violence of youth, of want, and children laughing, skipping beneath the curtain call of this world—then we wouldn't cling to life so. There would be no use for memory. We would rise to eat, lie in the sun, then sleep again until it was all over. It's beauty that has grown our minds. And it is beauty that has undone us. For a long time, I have wondered whether it would exist without the end, without death. If beauty and death are coincident, codependent. I still wonder now.

4.

I question whether Madera realizes that this is the loneliest of activities—going on about myself to myself, morning after morning. It would be better if there were someone I could call, someone I could meet for tea, someone with me to say *Mmhmm* or *Huh* or *Oh, my!* But at a certain point in an old person's life, those people we might like to waste an entire afternoon with have either crossed to the other side or lived so long absent from our lives that they might as well be dead.

There were so many girls I might still know, girls I knew in New York, ones with whom I'd go ice skating, girls who sat beside me in French or Latin at Hunter College High School, and we'd go on and on and on about whom we might marry and where we might marry and what we might wear to marry, and then once we were all married we would exchange letters, just a few, until time was the only thing that passed between us. Oh, true, there were women in town here on Lyra whom I'd meet weekly for tea at Tilly's; we'd speak of holidays, our plans for them, who was coming and what we would cook, holidays that were still months away. When one had passed, we'd start talking about the next. Thanksgiving and then Christmas, Christmas and then New Year's, New Year's and then so much emptiness. For a time, I was very popular on the island. My diary was full from Monday to Friday with lunches, lunches that lasted for hours. Those women—what were all their names? It doesn't matter now. Never did we exchange one true word. And yet we squandered so much of this life together.

One woman's face from that ancient Rolodex materializes from my memory, and yet I could swear it was only the once, in that lonely initial winter on Lyra, that I ever encountered its owner. The first brush of cold was not so devastating as it had been in New York, when come October the heat left overnight, without hesitation or regret. Lyra was kinder. It stayed light later and warmed almost to summer during the day. But Gabriel had just died, and so it was inexplicably cold. And I was pregnant with my first child, so I felt frigid even beneath the blazing sun. The world was gutted; all I could see were its dark parts. Was it the eccentric aspect of the stranger herself that implanted her face so firmly in my mind, or the spell of time from which she arose? I do not know if memory works like the planets and stars in space: the heavier a season, the more time slows around it.

There was snow that year, and the dunes were a wonder against the dark-blue Atlantic. All the magnolia leaves dropped, the palmettos were murdered by frost, and the moss was subsumed by icicles. We were accused by some of having brought the north and its weather with us. This woman was one of them, that day in December, just sitting down with me like a guest on one of our chairs on the beach, where I had come to hide over my lunch.

"Don't reckon we've ever met," she said casually, as if I were the one trespassing on her property.

I was too young or too sad or too shy or too lonely or mostly too curious to consider reprimanding her. "Can't I get you anything?" I asked. In her lap, she clutched a red picnic basket and an umbrella.

"Oh, no, ma'am." She shook her head dramatically. "Up here, you've got the best view of the ocean in all the island. You know that? I'm content to just look at it."

"Doesn't it look the same here as anywhere else?" I asked.

"You can't see how it shows its face right here?" she replied.

"What face are you referring to?" I asked.

"The ocean's," she said. "Look closely. You can see, between the swells, that the ocean is dreaming something nice."

"I'm sorry, Miz . . ." I said, waiting for her to fill in the rest of her title, but the woman never offered a name. "I don't believe I understand."

The woman was mad, certainly, but she did not frighten me. I wanted to hear her go on and on, deeper into that dimension which did not quite resemble our own, but rather the realm of a child's imagination. And she did go on and on, her voice mingling with the hush of the sea, until, unbelievably, hours had passed, and spurred by a polite glance at my watch, I was forced out of the reverie her tales had sewn around me. ". . . so many of 'em drowned after gazing down into the depths at the ocean gems. It's because you can see the beginning of the whole universe in those stones."

"I'm so very sorry," I broke in. "It was nice chatting with you, but I must finish up here and get ready for our guests." Joseph, Simon's brother, was arriving that evening.

She ignored this and trained her gaze back toward the ocean. "Prettiest things you ever saw, but you gotta swim into the *deep* deep to really see 'em. And then it gets too hard to come back. No one ever comes back. Why would you want to come back here after you've looked into the eyes of God?"

"I wouldn't know," I said, standing and wiping the sand from my skirt to emphasize my departure.

"You do know" was all she said, her eyes like an owl's, dramatic, unblinking.

Moments later, I was greeting Joseph's wife, Deborah, whom I had not yet met. "My husband always said Simon was the melodramatic type," she cooed as she gazed around our home. "But will you take a look at all this?"

Before I could answer, Deborah held her left hand up beside my own. Her engagement ring featured a diamond three times the size of the one Simon had given me. "Now, Elle, dear, which one do you think catches the light more?" She chuckled conspiratorially. "Sometimes I wonder whether I married my ring or my husband!"

Deborah was a beauty queen, from one of those New England families that struck gold the moment they set foot on Plymouth Rock. She was busty where I wasn't, red-haired and cat-eyed, and had a dancer's posture. Since childhood, I had always been reprimanded for slouching. "You mean to say you only have one maid here?" she went on. "But how do you ever keep it clean? I should send you one of ours. They never know what to do with themselves. They hate working, these people. You have to make them do it."

The conversation went on this way, on that same day that I'd learned of the ocean's capacity for dreams. Up in her room, as they settled in, Deborah rang the bell for Ethel's assistance every twenty minutes. I had not yet used it once. I was never trained in the ancient art of making others do what you can just as easily do for yourself.

"I hope you don't still feel you got the short end of the stick being sent here," Joseph said to Simon that night at dinner. Simon's brother had sturdy hands and a broad chest from playing quarterback in his youth. Simon had never performed anything more athletic than a brisk walk. Joseph's suits were perfectly tailored to him; Simon's jackets devoured his frame. Still, Joseph was the sort of man who by age forty would grow fat. His voice was like that of a petty king, with the haughty command of one who considered himself the most important person at any table. "It's quite the opportunity. You know, I felt a little sore when Father proposed it to you instead of me."

"The weather is good for me." Simon regarded his brother with a gaze that mere mortals reserved for their gods.

"So they say. Couldn't tell from tonight, though. It's colder than New York."

"The property is nice, isn't it?" Simon asked.

"A real jewel in the jungle," Deborah chirped. Joseph cast a glance her way for the first and only time that evening, a look that meant *Shut that pretty, fatuous mouth*.

"You're starting to speak like one of them, Simon. Is there anyone here who's educated enough to talk numbers?" Joseph asked when he was finished silently humiliating his wife.

"I meet with the mayor of the island now and again. Educated at Harvard. Elle's not much for it. She's never worried herself about these things." Simon giggled. Now we were even, Deborah and me.

"Ain't that the fellow we bought this swamp from? You and Father are always too impressed by these Ivy League types," Joseph replied, throttling Simon's mirth. "In my experience they're know-it-all good-for-nothings. Surprised an island this size even has a mayor. Why, you should be the mayor, given the charity we're doing employing all these people during a war. What's he call himself again?"

"Clarke. Old family, around these parts," Simon replied.

"And how is it going—the prospect?" Joseph asked, swatting away a bug that had become caught in a flying pattern around his face.

"Very promising," Simon said. "We'll be drowning in it in no time."

Joseph pounded Simon's back as if the mosquito had just landed there to meet its death. "We better be. We're getting murdered in diamonds. Can't believe those damn South Africans have got every gal in heat for them with one little shred of ad copy. But they'll get tired of diamonds once the war's over and their husbands are lavishing them on their French whores, too. A good American wife'll want this blue, this blue—"

"Wonder?" I offered, but everyone seemed to have temporarily gone deaf. "If you'll excuse me," I said, to obliterate my attempt at poetry, "I feel as though I'm going to be ill."

One nice thing about being a mere woman in my day was that one only had to threaten to feel faint or nauseated when one wanted to be discourteous. This was even easier while pregnant. As I got up from the table, they all expressed their tired hope that I was carrying a son. But she would be a girl.

I left the miserable party and snuck out through the service door into the yard. A storm had recently passed over Lyra. Its lightning had shorn the oak, and left the woods skeletal. But on that night there was no weather. The beach chair where my strange visitor had sat hours earlier, with her red picnic basket, was still and empty, deserted. The full moon was up and cast over the ocean, and I looked upon its glowing surface to see if I might glimpse any of its dreams. All I saw was a golden road into the black.

"When are you lost in now, Elle?" Simon asks. Suddenly I find we are sitting in the garden. It is no longer 1941. A newspaper is in my husband's lap. His front page is turned to me. The headlines: a blizzard in May, bombs kill scores in Haifa, a stock market collapse, a new virus born in the streets of Hong Kong. The fountain chokes, but no water falls from its spout. I ask if Elijah will ever fix it.

"You mean old Elijah, Elijah?" Simon looks at me peculiarly.

"What other Elijah is there?" I ask. I do not know what I have said wrong, so I tell Simon he'd better quit chewing his gum like a cow.

"It's better than smoking, Elle. The scientists say that kills you in a multitude of ways." I look down to find a cigarette in my hand.

"Since when have I cared about science?" I ask half facetiously.

"You used to love your astronomy books," he says. Then he turns the newspaper up to his face again. "No longer, I suppose. . . . I've always been fascinated by it."

"Well, it got you nowhere good, following Joe around. All those facts and figures," I say. "That's what that batty woman on the beach told me to watch out for. She was like a prophet. She had those owl's eyes."

"Say, Elle, maybe it's time you got a little shut-eye?"

5.

I fall into a dream of my garden, full of roses, the fountain whispering, the sky soft with spring light. Everything is young again, the land naïve. Time has not yet learned of its own passing. I open a door in the trunk of an oak tree to find a rainbow of silk. Hidden there are all my favorite dresses. But when I press a pearl number against my body, I realize that I've grown far older than this early season of the world. And then the rose blossoms brown and shrivel. Spring and then summer are gone. That cold November hue, its last cry of red, consumes all the trees. It is all so quick, so horrifying.

ONCE I AM AWAKE, it is still spring, and the wind has knocked from the bureau my mother's ceramic doll, the one she famously carried with her all the way across the ocean to America from Russia. Mina the cat is already attacking the shattered remainders and a bottle of pills that fell alongside it. I draw up the doll's pieces, the blue petals of her dress, the remainder of her limbs, her pathetic, fragile fingers.

Out the window, I see Simon in the garden, where I left him hours earlier, now in the company of my daughter. Their voices scale the wall to my room, animated or agitated, I cannot tell.

It is just May, and already even walking in the sun is like brushing against the devil's flesh. I'm not sure whether it's the oppressive heat or my poor mind, but as I cross the lawn toward my family, I can't locate the name my mother had for the doll. I almost hear my mother's voice pronounce it—that voice I have not heard since I was a child.

"We've already finished lunch," Simon announces to me.

"And I've got to get going soon," my daughter says. "Gordon's gotten into a bit of trouble."

Blue Rose is older than your own old mother. Blue Rose will live forever. Blue Rose, Blue Rose—

"When is your husband not in trouble?" Simon asks.

But will you live forever, Mama?

My mouth goes to greet my daughter, but her name blurs beneath Blue Rose the doll, and the oak and its rainbow trunk of silk . . .

"Elle, it's Zelda," she says, taking my hand.

"Why do you insist on this first-name business?" Simon asks angrily. "That's your mother. Is this something Gordon taught you, too?"

"Of course I know it's you, you silly girl," I reply.

But then my mother's name returns to me: *Sanya*. My mouth moves over its sounds. My father whispered it in his sleep after she was dead of an otherwise unextraordinary seasonal flu. *Sanya Sanya Sanya.*

"Sanya?" Zelda asks. "Who's Sanya?"

Simon looks at Zelda. "I assume she's referring to your long-dead grandmother."

"I've just come to visit with you both," I say. Zelda wraps her arms in mine as if to escort me somewhere. "There was an accident and Blue Rose—"

"We sold the ship, Elle," Simon says. "Remember?"

"The ship from Russia? No, Simon, that's long gone," I say. "I mean the doll in my room. She fell to the floor, and is broken to pieces. I dreamt and I woke up and—"

"Mother, isn't it time for your nap?" Zelda asks.

"But I've just woken up. I just told you that."

"Well, you must be a bit chilled. Why don't you go on up and get a shawl," she says, pushing me back toward the porch, even though it's absolutely scorching. Once they have me back inside, Zelda slams the garden door in my face, and within moments they are shouting again.

"Simon, you'll die on this stupid island. All alone in this big house with no one to help you. Not even Ray."

"The business isn't dead yet," Simon shouts back. "And please stop calling me Simon!"

"With all due respect, Simon, which business are you speaking of? Your treasure hunt that died thirty years ago? Or that pharmaceutical hoax—"

"How dare you, Zelda," Simon growls. "Repeating those accusations. That tabloid trash. I am your *father.* That husband of yours has made you forget your class."

"Leave Gordon out of this. It's not just the media. Joe and Deb told me about the recall, Dad."

"Caeruleum is as safe as water—when it's pure, Zelda. It was Joe's crew of geniuses who got us into this godforsaken mess."

"We are going in circles," Zelda shouts. "My question is, why do you still need all this?" She gazes up at the house. "Why don't you sell the place, get out of here before the island turns into a ghost town?"

"And I suppose Gordon wouldn't mind gambling away the proceeds of our estate, too?" Simon shouts back.

I almost scream: But who will sit in the parlor at the grand piano if not Simon? Whose portrait will hang in the living room, if not my own, that twenty-three-year-old face gazing into the distance, the garden, the woods, into the opaque future? Whose china will quiver in the seconds before a hurricane makes landfall, our own sirens of late summer? I want to tell Zelda I can hear her still, scrambling up and down the staircases, sliding on her knees. Every birthday party, every holiday, the aroma of cocoa, of popcorn, of roasted meat. Come Christmas, we lit up every tree in the yard. This house is all that remains of time for me. There was some happiness here, after all.

But I say nothing. I tiptoe down the front stairs. Spider mites have finished off the rosebushes that once adorned the path from the drive. Their ghostly webs brew a temporary fog. My house is passing away with me. I go farther, leaving my daughter, my husband, my garden, for the relentless oak. There is always a moment in the woods when I wonder if I will ever see it again, the ocean—and then there it is, that shimmer. I make my way to the top of a dune to rest, and just for a second I close my eyes. Sometimes it is too much, the sea. Sometimes I can't bear to look at it all at once.

When I open my eyes again, it is as if he has been waiting there all afternoon. Gabriel looks at me frankly, hand on his hip, his stance either agitation or boredom. That old emotion returns: I am riotous with desire. My pathetic veins burn with it. Gabriel walks toward me, his hand stretched out for mine. I am all over again young. I pinch his ear with my thumb and pointer finger, to greet him. It was our way on Lyra. We could pretend we were truly cousins inside such a small gesture.

"Elle Bell, how long have you been stranded here?" Dusk falls, and its palette lingers, intimating the halls of eternity. The ocean is thin and sweet as a lake. It is the water of some other place and I want to swim in it at last. Gabriel looks at me expectantly. Beyond him I see a boat, waiting there for us to board. He cups my chin affectionately in his hand, those large, rough fingers I haven't seen in so long, nails mired with grime. His eyes swirl as if they've consumed the stars. "As always with dreams," he says, "you can't take a photograph of this."

Then he sweeps his arms out at the view.

"Elle, Mayor Clarke's wife is here!" The music stops. The afternoon resumes in its bright, casual light. I am not on the beach but lying in my own bed.

"Did you see him?" I shriek.

"Simon is in town," Ethel says. "Mrs. Clarke insists y'all have an appointment together. It's half past three now."

"With Zelda?" I ask.

"That was yesterday Miss Zelda paid us a visit," Ethel replies. "Zelda left yesterday."

Downstairs, Mrs. Clarke talks into a phone that has no cord, the technology of which I presumably should understand but do not. Whoever is on the other end apparently cannot hear her very well, as she is screaming into it like a ghoul in a nightmare, swatting her hands around her wedding cake updo, which has drawn to it a few of the season's largest lovebugs.

I sit at the table across from her for some time before she hollers: "Goodbye! I have to go now. I'm sitting here with Elle Ranier. I said I have to go now." After several minutes more of this, she disconnects the call.

"Now, Elle, I'm here to talk business, girl to girl. Like we used to do."

There are two cups on the table. I reach for one hesitantly. Mrs. Clarke reaches for the other and puts it to her mouth. I don't know if I should hold mine, set it down, or do as she has done. What is to be done with the cup? I want her to be quiet, and I hope this is the way it is done, with the cup affixed to her mouth.

"Your tea will get cold," Ethel whispers to me as Mrs. Clarke keeps talking.

"You know it's not Christian to indulge in gossip," Mrs. Clarke continues. "If you recall, the last time I came to you about anything unseemly, it was when Ray got his hands into too many liquor cabinets and was becoming a proper devil to our island. Well, that's all water under the bridge—we hear Ray's found the Lord's righteous path at last. Oh, shame on me for digging up old wounds. To get right down to it, Elle, the reason I'm here is there's been a little worm about this business of taking the Caeruleum off the market. But the mining will go on still, right? There's got to be some other use for the site. Pay was a week late last month and we very nearly had a riot—"

I raise the cup and hold it out over the table, signifying my turn to speak. "Excuse me, dear," I cut in. "Did you happen to see a young man come through here? He was just there on the beach—"

"Oh, my, do you think one of 'em was trying to rob you? You know how they turn heathen when they don't get their pay, Elle." She looks quickly at Ethel, then away.

Ethel interrupts her. "The missus hasn't been feeling like herself today. Maybe you ought to come back another time."

"I certainly will." Mrs. Clarke sets her cup back on the table, puts her handkerchief over her mouth, then plugs her nose. "These lovebugs are spreading a plague that comes from Mexico, you know. I heard it on the radio today. Folks are falling sick and dying. At first it just feels like the flu. . . ." Before departing, the cordless telephone reattaches itself to her cheek. Half talking into it, she says: "Oh, Mary Louise, you heard about these damn Mexicans, right?" and then to me, her voice trailing off at last: "You'd better make certain to see the doctor, Elle, just in case you caught it."

6.

It was still in New York City, some June long gone, fireflies rising and falling out of the trees—when Gabriel first introduced me to the lovebug. I was more mesmerized by the swarm all around us, their mimetic starlight, than by Gabriel's nervous chatter. "Did you know, Elle, there's an insect down in New Orleans that kisses each other just like we do?"

Gabriel's hand rested on the small of my back, then slipped down beneath the band of my skirt. I slapped him there and he went on. "I'm serious—the bugs, the male and the female ones, can't live without each other. They never go unattached. They're just always together, literally stuck to each other, making love until they die," he said. With his knuckles, he mocked the movement of his fantastical bugs.

"Is that right, Professor Bell?" I asked. "And what about why the fireflies light up like that?" I was still more interested in the biosphere all around us. As it turned out, his lovebug was real flesh and blood, too, though I didn't know it then. His lovebugs would only manifest themselves in droves later, here on Lyra.

"Those aren't lightning bugs, Elle, they're fairies," he said. "They'll be even prettier in there." Gabriel gestured toward the entrance to Green-Wood Cemetery. He had been searching all night, in the way that young men do, for a place to be adequately alone with me. I never knew where Gabriel called home. Perhaps he came by his familiarity with the city's outdoor secrets because he found his bed so often in a park or on the beach or beneath a bridge.

I pleaded with him not to enter the graveyard. "It's forecast to rain, Gabriel!"

"I've not only come prepared with an umbrella, I've even brought us a five-course supper in this red picnic basket," he said and slipped through the iron lattice, his body passing without effort. "And a sweet little French Bordeaux," he said, whipping a bottle from his pocket.

"Where are you going?" I shouted into the dark. "Come back!"

His pale face emerged again. "I've met a ghost, Elle."

"I don't believe in ghosts," I countered.

"Don't you want to hear what the ghost has to say?" he replied. "You'll have to come in here to find out."

The trees in the cemetery shivered in the wind. Graveyards always harbored that hush, the hush of deserts and oceans, of the places on the planet where the violence of the living is disbanded. Sex lived beside death, too, and I felt it draw shapes along my skin when I finally joined Gabriel. It was true—the fireflies were everywhere, winking light on the grassy knolls between graves. There were no lamps, no lanterns. The moon had set. The night was ours, a secret we shared with those glittering bugs.

"Now that you're here, I can tell you," Gabriel said. "I've seen what heaven looks like, Elle. The ghost has shown me."

I felt I might begin to hate him for this line of conversation, morbid as it was foolish, but then he drew me into him, whispering fairy tales in my ear, and I was wrangled back into our love—our summer solstice forever, our dreamscape sea.

"What the ghost told me is that heaven is here among us, only we can't see it. These trees aren't full of bugs—those are blue and violet lights, crawling through the branches and on into the sky. And that pond just there? Well, if you swam in it, rather than little fishes you'd see stars."

"And how did this person die, the one who's now your ghost?" I asked.

"For love," Gabriel answered. "The woman he loved married another. He was a poor man and couldn't care for her, so he drowned himself."

"Your ghost committed suicide rather than look for work?" I asked. "How very romantic of him."

I pulled myself out of Gabriel's arms. I was no lovebug; we were only human. I stumbled away toward the pond—with its celestial stars or goldfish—and considered one possible future: that in the years to come I'd receive a letter saying Gabriel had died in the war we were not yet in, but would be soon enough. I saw his body, the one I loved, bloody and at rest on a cliff in France. In my youth, I was intoxicated by the velvet promise of tragedy, of how adult it could make me feel. There is a certain competition for the weight of experience that only the inexperienced desire. Still, I wonder now if that moment, and the others like it, sprang only from my penchant for melodrama. Have I always craved sadness? Or did I know, from the very moment I met him, that we would be parted too soon?

Gabriel chased after me, breaking my reverie, and we tumbled to our knees against a tree, its bark drawing pinpoints of blood.

"You've hurt me, Gabriel Bell," I chided.

"I am the ghost," Gabriel said, his mouth already passing over the shaded places on my body, "who exists to haunt you."

THE DAWN WAS STUNNING that morning, a heartbreak of red, when at last I snuck back into our apartment just before my father rose for work. I was too intoxicated by love to sleep. The smell of burned coffee and the smell of Gabriel return to me from that long-ago kitchen. I brought my nails to my nose to remind myself of him, of what we had done, of the earth and the sweat and the mammal of him, the scents that only lovers love. When my father awoke, I shoved my hands into two oven mitts, as if he could smell on me what I could smell on myself. The apartment was so small, the windows in it fit for a prison cell, but in that sliver of an opening, the sunrise was still ostentatious, symphonic. But when I looked up at my father's face, I saw that it had aged ten years in a night.

"I'm glad you're awake, Ellie," my father said. "There's something I want to discuss with you." Suddenly tumbling forth from his face was a great sob. I had never seen the man cry.

"I'm so sorry, Papa," I wailed, figuring he knew where I had been, what I had done.

"Elle," he said, calming me, petting my hair. "Sorry for what? It's me that's sorry. I've been a failure all of my life. The only thing I didn't fail at was marrying your mother, and she would have done better to avoid me. But that's all spilt milk." He forced a smile. "I've been meaning to tell you . . . You're a woman now, Elle, and a very pretty one. We can marry you well." He suddenly became sheepish, as if he'd just won a match against an invisible opponent. He looked at me with tenderness, his eyes the color of cedar. "There's a man . . ." He swallowed, then continued. "My boss, Ranier—you know how wealthy he is, he's got more jewels in his house than a prince, and though I know all these years I've only been his shopkeeper, well, he has a son named Simon who's in need of a wife. Apparently, this Simon saw you once when you came to fetch your old father, and I'm told he fell in love on the spot."

Here was my punishment for being with Gabriel out of wedlock. The penalty had come. "Oh, well, Father, I'm sure Mr. Ranier was only trying to give you a compliment," I said, anxious to dodge the inevitable.

"Ranier's let me go, Ellie. I'm too old for the work. And he needs someone to do more of the heavy lifting, is what he says." The decades had settled upon my father. It was not just his face that had aged, but his shoulders had shriveled. He had shrunk, and what hair of his he still had left was white. If time could defeat my father, it would defeat us all. Everything ends, I thought then. We fall from the branch, disintegrate. There is no explosion. We don't burst into light. Our smell becomes rot.

"But it doesn't matter anymore, you see?" my father continued. "Don't you worry, oh my child. Once you're married, we'll both be taken care of. We've always been a team, haven't we?"

I still hear him saying it, *oh my child*, the way one reaches for the sound of the ocean inside a seashell. "Everything will be all right. Mr. Simon's in love with you, my Ellie. And Mr. Ranier, when he let me go, he says to me, 'How 'bout it, Cumberland? Now you can really be a part of the Ranier family.' Oh my child, why do you cry? I'm giving you away to the American dream!"

7.

A soft rain raps against all the windows of Lyra. The entire house is enchanted by the weather's lullaby and the aroma of butter wafting through it from Ethel's biscuits. I sit at the table salivating for my meal, like every hungry mammal the world over. Simon, on the other hand, sits observing me as if awaiting my answer to some mysterious question about the origin of the universe.

"Are you waiting for me to say something?" I ask him at last.

"I've asked you three times already, and every time I do, you gaze toward the window like I'm not here at all!" Simon shouts.

I spend my days this way now, hunting the passageways for his words. I am looking for their echoes, those scrambling cubs, disappearing over the edge of existence, when Ethel appears.

"If she can't hear me, maybe you can," Simon says, turning toward Ethel. "Ethel, I asked my wife if, after all I have done for her—this house, all her diamonds, her beautiful dresses, her pearls, her designer shoes, her silk sheets, all the money I ever made on this godforsaken island, all for her—I asked if she's ever been anything but sad here."

"Mr. Simon," Ethel says, taken aback, and then sets down the biscuits, hunting for the rest of her sentence. "She's sick."

"She's been sick since the day I met her," Simon says calmly, then stands up, smooths his tie. "I did everything. Everything I could. All I ever did was for her. And now they want to crucify me for it."

"Simon," I protest, but manage to say nothing else.

"I'm off to meet Raymond," he says. "Apparently, we are the only ones left who wish to save this entire cursed enterprise." Then the front door slams behind him.

Ethel sits at the table in Simon's absence. The biscuits are devoured before either of us speaks and it is Ethel who disrupts the hush of the rain. "Sometimes I don't miss having a husband. All men do is complain, complain, complain. They just remember the bad things. Like Mr. Simon doesn't remember all those times you wore a pretty smile on your face as his belligerent associates got drunk as the devil, carousing right under your nose. You ever think we'd just be better off without men? We should be teaching our girls to use them for all ten minutes they're worth, then be done for good with all their selfishness."

"They just take all our strength and grace," I reply. "And leave nothing behind."

A soft rain fell, too, on that first day my father escorted me down Ninety-seventh Street toward Riverside Drive. "Strength and grace, Ellie," my father said before leaving me in the lobby of the Raniers' building. "Don't be nervous. Just show up with your strength and grace. There isn't a hair on your head Mr. Simon won't love."

In the elevator to the penthouse, my chest constricted. Just past the fifth floor, the elevator suffered a bump in its ascent. Some poor soul who now haunted the thing he'd helped build, perhaps, or some teenage bride who never dreamed of being a wife. And then the doors opened directly into the apartment. Simon was seated at the piano beside a large window that revealed the breadth of the Hudson, lost in a melody I didn't then recognize. I was never educated in music. He did not seem to have noticed that I'd arrived. His eyes were closed, his long delicate fingers danced across the keys—this, my first image of him. The song went on for half an hour, it seemed. He turned to me when it was over and his eyes opened, a breathtaking lapis beneath long black eyelashes, brimming with tears. "Miss Cumberland," he said. "Excuse me—it is just sacrilege to cut Rachmaninoff short. Are you familiar with his work?"

To this day I do not know if his emotions were a response to the music or to my presence. What I do remember is that I felt as though the entire house had eyes and they were scrutinizing me.

Suddenly I could not bear the sight of my hideous shoes. They were the color of urine from wear, and here they were mucking up the oriental carpet, adorned with scenes of princes charging toward their princesses in some radiant past. I was so caught up in my shame that I wondered whether, if I were to tuck one foot behind another beautifully, the way a ballerina does in sous-sous, the house might permit the monstrosity of my shoes.

As I stood there, paralyzed by self-consciousness, I did not notice that Simon's mother was standing in the entryway of the parlor. The house's eyes belonged to its mistress, after all. "Are you trained in ballet, Miss Cumberland?" she asked. Her gaze performed a grand sweep of me.

"Mrs. Ranier," I said, instinctively flattening my skirt. I understood that what would follow was a kind of audition, even perhaps an interrogation.

"You are beautiful, it's true," she said. I had passed part of the test, then, though Mrs. Ranier's eyes still ranged over me. She asked questions at speed, without waiting for my answers. I might as well have been standing there naked.

"Simon's older brother, Joseph, and their father send their regards. They are still at the office. Simon is more like me. He prefers entertainment to paperwork." She walked over to her son and rested her hand on his shoulder. "Are you a Rachmaninoff aficionada, Miss Cumberland?"

I nodded my head, silent and eager as a fool.

"I've brought you a small present." She had been holding a sizable box in her hands the entire time. I opened it: a fur coat, its scent recalling French perfume, Russian courts, ancient Egypt, Cleopatra and Marie Antoinette. "It's just a small mink," she said. "Go ahead—try it on."

It was gorgeous—but so much so that my shoes seemed all the more hideous. I wished to have my very feet amputated. Even more embarrassing, we had not boiled water in the apartment that morning, so I had not been able to bathe. My odor, I was sure, would sully the smell of the coat. I slipped out of it quickly, but I already missed it. It was in that coat that I first felt the assurance that comes with money, the way it falls on a body.

"Do you not fancy it?" Mrs. Ranier asked.

I tried to rearrange my face into an expression of aloofness, as if I had hundreds of such items waiting for me in apartments across New York City. "It fits like a glove, but I've been perspiring on account of the . . . the fire," I said, pinpointing a culprit for the coat's sudden removal.

"Simon insists on baking this room. He's the only one of us who enjoys the heat. Well, I have so many more things that would just look splendid on you, Miss Cumberland. I lost my figure after childbirth and my dresses are wasted on me. It is an understatement, on the other hand, to say you are quite the lovely creature." Mrs. Ranier then pulled Simon up from his happier place at the piano and nudged him forward, toward me. "Simon, Miss Cumberland looks like she would enjoy a walk beside the river. Wouldn't you, my dear?"

Outside, Simon held his umbrella over me, allowing the rain to fall freely on his own beautiful suit. "My mother always forces gifts on people. I rather wish she wouldn't. Don't you think it's better to choose one's own presents?"

I was embarrassed to speak, to reveal my inadequacy on the subject. "I suppose, if given the choice," I said finally, almost inaudibly, wishing the rain could speak in my place.

"If given the choice, it is always better to have what one desires rather than what someone else desires for you."

Had this conversation occurred years later, I might have understood it from Simon's perspective. As it was, it took all of me just to nod in agreement rather than gush the name of the one who truly occupied my heart. Thankfully, we soon returned to Simon's apartment building, where, without much grace, he took my hand. "Well, are you interested in this business of courtship?"

Hours later, my legs were wrapped around Gabriel, as he rode me on his bicycle through the rain, that rain which still has not let up, which taps against my windows until now. His body against mine remained a mystery—the freckles of his neck that disappeared down his clothed back, the stubble of his chin, those eyes that undid my propriety. Where were we going, on that day in particular? Gabriel was riding me away from all inevitabilities. All that wind in my face, my rain-soaked clothes, my clamorous heart, my bright face passing through the streets of New York like a comet—this is my image of freedom still. We were flying.

The rain quiets to a trickle. What remains is my garden, which sleeps surrounding me. Moss clings to the oaks like the parasite time. Mosquitoes take turns piercing my legs. Mina the cat sleeps beside me, dreaming of savannas in Africa. It is near dusk, that most luscious of hours. Ethel has left for the evening. She must be walking against the blackening night along the river shore, where the light from the west lasts longest. Simon never returned after this morning's outburst. The ugly moments always remain, scattering craters across my disintegrating canvas. It is everything sweet that goes. Presumably Simon is out trying to save his empire. He is too old now to be with one of his lovers, back in Gabriel's abandoned shed, where he took them to protect my honor and his own. I am certain that an indecent amount of our money went to keeping them silent. I hope a few truly returned his affection.

The ocean beckons me with its mighty drone. I wish only to lie on its surface and float beneath the moon—examine its face, its ridges, its valleys, the crashes it, too, has suffered. In the early years, after Gabriel drowned, I stepped into the sea when it seemed to be at rest, breathing only barely, releasing a trembling wave every minute or so. I told myself: *At last you will not be afraid.* Gabriel had taught me once how to float—*Just lie on your back, let your legs dangle*—but when I lay down, I fell through the water's glass surface.

An arm clawed me out from shore, tumbled, then choked me. Nonetheless, the ocean decided it still did not want me. Another wave pushed me just as forcefully back to earth. I lay coughing on the sand until morning, watching the constellations rise and set beyond the moon. I'd again been in the water that had buried Gabriel. I had again drunk in his body. It was his grip in the tug of those waves, the same grip of his hands around my waist on the bicycle, in the animal embrace of love. *You can never leave me. Love comes only once in ten thousand years.* But he had let me go.

Rather than to the sea, I return to the house—the house that still smells of butter and rain, that still echoes Gabriel's voice from ten thousand years in the past—to find my husband storming through the door. His face is red, his breath syrupy from drinking. "Joseph removed me from the trust!"

"What trust?" I ask.

Simon storms down the hall away from me, the tantrum of this morning not finished or resolved. "Not you, not right now," he says, waving his hands in my face. He walks into his office and picks up the phone. "Raymond!" he screams into it.

For the second time in a day, I have made him impatient. Rather than pursue him any further, I think back instead to the ghost bride in Simon's elevator—the one that made that little bump when I passed floor five—and my father's mantra of *strength and grace*. But that elevator, my father's voice, the wind in my hair on that bicycle with Gabriel, all live so very long ago, and I more and more among them.

8.

Off toward the tree line, a sudden shimmer. It travels the arms of the oak the way lightning re-creates the sky. To get a closer look, I walk out onto the porch, where Simon's voice is only intermittent, a signal drowned by distance. The faraway light appears at first to consume only our garden, but the beams spread until the entire wood is illuminated before me, into an unearthly, faultless blue. The reflection glimmers in the rain puddles, pregnant with fireflies, fallen stars.

"Where have you gone to now, Elle?" I didn't hear Simon's eavesdropping footsteps. I suppose he has grown used to the light all around us. To him, it must be as common as the moon. I have only forgotten how to name such a wonder.

"I'm right here," I reply with little confidence. "Looking at the stars."

"Stars?" Simon asks. "The fog is thick as a pig."

"That one," I say timidly, pointing to the stilled firework, a waterfall of light pouring through the largest and most gravity-ridden oak in the yard.

"The stars." Simon laughs. It is all very funny to him, his little old wife pointing to nothing in the dark. What, then, explains this shining—bright and pretty as the galaxies fallen to Earth? I understand my brain is rotting, that my memories are disappearing beneath the cover of time, like shells being ripped off the shore and rolled back into the ocean. But no doctor ever mentioned this. A voice emerges from the dark. *As always with dreams . . .*

"You can't take a photograph of this," I recite, though I cannot place where I've heard the words before.

"A photograph of what?" Simon asks.

"What's that?" I ask.

"Let's go in, Elle. I can play something for you. Whatever you would like to hear." The day's persistent rain returns in big fat drops. "Tomorrow, if the road isn't flooded, perhaps we can go into town."

"Oh, that would be very nice. I can get some tea at Tilly's," I say, hardly aware I am responding. I have said the same words a thousand times before: *To Tilly's, maybe stop by the florist.*

"Tilly's is gone, Elle," Simon says, reaching for me. "As is the florist." Liver spots have sprouted all over his knuckles. His hands are pale, papery, withered. These are not my husband's hands. I look at his face for some confirmation, and there are his eyes, the color of the Atlantic. Simon is still here.

"Ah, yes, yes." I nod my head. "Of course." But how is Tilly's closed? I have been there every Tuesday for all time. A faintness arises, like an Impressionist's painting, a blur. The building where

Tilly's was, its sign taken down. And then one day there was a new sign. But nothing ever opened there again. The past is all shuttered. My old paths are darkening. The lights in the windows have long since burned out.

"Simon," I say matter-of-factly. "Everything on the island is closing, isn't it?"

"The rain's begun," he replies, as though I can no longer perceive even the weather.

I follow him inside. I am his wife: all these years spent following him back inside our house. Simon sits down at the piano and taps the bench beside him. "Come sit, my belle."

"What's happened to the business, Simon?" I ask.

His hands crawl across the piano. He is already living in his music, far away. "You know what tomorrow is, right?"

I yearn to know the answer. I hunt every aching corner of my brain. If only he will quit that bombastic melody, I can concentrate enough to find it. But moments begin to pass. My gaze wanders again toward the window on the garden, where the shimmer still haunts the trees, a new life form subsuming all the tired, mortal leaves in the universe. *Those aren't lightning bugs, Elle, they're fairies.*

"Tomorrow's your birthday, Elle." Simon sighs and closes the piano's fallboard. "It's the Fourth of July."

PART 2

Summer

9.

It was on the Fourth of July so soon after we met that I was engaged to Simon. That midsummer day of my twentieth birthday, it drizzled an autumn rain. The clouds were swollen white, the sort that might change their minds and drop clumps of snow. On my way up to Simon's apartment that afternoon, the elevator compartment rattled violently and its little lamp sputtered out. I fell to my knees. For a moment, I hung there, suspended so many stories high in the shaft. Then, using a match, I recovered my body in the dark. The tiny fire must have alerted whoever was my guardian angel, as the elevator soon began to rise again.

Perhaps only the dead can move forward and backward in time, and it was my own future ghost conspiring against me in that elevator, because as soon as the doors opened into that most beautiful apartment in all of New York City, I knew what was to come. It was as if I'd seen it all before, in a dream or another life.

Simon would kneel on the carpet beside the piano, the same one that weeks before had been the backdrop for my monstrous shoes. A ship's horn would sound; the trains along the Hudson would grumble on toward their next stop, intimating the illusion of escape. And in his hands, Simon would have his birthday present for me. I would look not at his face, but into the eyes of the diamond, a ring that would contain the glory of this world and the impossible next.

And so it was, all of it. I never had to say yes. I just didn't say no. I let him place the ring on my finger. And it was done.

Mrs. Ranier entered the parlor seconds later, watching the whole engagement transpire from some hidden spy quarters. Simon turned to her for approval, as if it were to his mother he had proposed. "That gem is one of our very best, cut from a stone far superior to anything the competition claims to have," she exclaimed. "Have you seen their ridiculous recent advertisements?"

I shook my head that I hadn't, though their name was suddenly everywhere in those days; they had hired every starlet in Hollywood to wear a diamond of theirs the size of a knuckle.

"Well, it's silly to discuss such things at a thrilling time for us all." Sincere tears formed in her eyes when she embraced me. "I know you lost your mother very young, Elle, so I hope you'll consider me as your own."

I was too humble or too numb to reply appropriately, but I recall managing an awkward curtsy, unconsciously acknowledging for us both the end of a certain stage act between us and the beginning of a new one.

Back below Canal Street, my father was sitting in the living room staring out the window grimly. "How was Mr. Ranier today?" he asked as soon as I entered, his face brightening slightly at the very mention of Simon.

I flashed my newly glittering hand indignantly. But my father still erupted in tears of joy, which soon afterward devolved into a fit of violent coughing. The smell in the apartment had changed with my father unemployed; it was the smell of age taking command of a man. This was the essential cruelty at the heart of life, that even the wildest roses stank of death toward their ends.

"You foolish thing," my father said when he was thoroughly exhausted from his outburst. His face for an instant resumed the sharpness of youth, the face I'd seen in old photographs of the time just before I was born. He trained his eyes on me with the naïveté of a particularly American conviction. "Don't you see, this is the happiest day of your life?"

"What's the difference between this and working in a brothel?" I shouted.

"Elle, I'm living only for you. My days are numbered. How do you expect to go on?" my father asked me. "I've fought to protect you from the reality out there, despite my poverty. The entire world is a brothel. Especially for an unmarried woman. Far worse than you can ever imagine. No man will guard you from it like Simon Ranier can."

That same evening, Gabriel and I had planned to meet in the alleyway beside a nearby bakery, but when I arrived Gabriel was not there. I searched for some time, up and down the dark avenue, trying to appear composed. I was growing ever more conscious of the drunken cries of strangers emanating from every direction, my father's talk of brothels reverberating inside my head, when at last I heard a burst of laughter ring out from across the street. Gabriel emerged from behind a lamppost.

I screamed at Gabriel that he was truly rotten. Spotting my hand as he crossed the street, he took it when he reached me. "What's this? Are you marrying the king of England?"

"It was my grandmother's," I lied. "Father let me wear it for my birthday."

"Was your grandmère married to the king of France?" Gabriel asked.

"Yes," I replied. "And I'm engaged to his son."

"Isn't that incest?" Gabriel asked, plucking at the gift of Mrs. Ranier's. "And why don't you let this fur hibernate? It's July. Who is it giving you all of these fancy things, Elle? I swear I saw that same ring recently in a gentlemen's magazine."

"My father's boss just leaves these things around the shop. Don't ask me why, Gabriel. You know how rich people are. They tire of even the nicest things."

"Even they don't grow sick of diamond rings, Elle."

"How would you know anything about it?" I challenged. At this, Gabriel dropped his inquest and pulled my arm into the night. The streets were empty except for a few select drunks leaving the bars with their female companions, stumbling and slurring through one patriotic song after another. It was true that the temperature had risen. July had returned, cloying and warm. We walked toward the water for the breeze, and, upon reaching it, Gabriel ran to the river's edge and threw the anchor off a rather expensive-looking boat. Furiously he worked at its sail, despite my screams of objection, until it was some ten feet from shore.

Gabriel's outline had already disappeared into the blackness when the first firework burst into the sky, followed by a stream of brilliant, falling light. One after another he set them off from the boat; his face reappeared with each burst, cast in violet, then blue, then red, mesmerized by his own magic trick. Some of those fireworks died between the shore and the boat, extinguished between our mortal bodies in that river, and some have lasted forever until now.

I ran into the water, toward him, with the blind courage of love.

He would steal the boat, I thought; he would sail me all the way to China. *Like we could go somewhere.*

"Watch out for sharks!" Gabriel shouted.

"There aren't any sharks in the river!" I cried. The water was up to my knees. I could not get to him without swimming. Suddenly every weed was a vicious fin lashing my calves.

"Then why do you look so scared?" he taunted me, then dove off the boat and disappeared into the water.

10.

Zelda reemerges from a swim in the ocean, patches of gray streaked through her drying hair, her mouth tightened into a frown, a war trench etched between her eyebrows. Ever since she was a wee thing, she has paced this way, back and forth in laps along the coastline. I was always jealous of her little body, buoyed up by the waves, then dipping and disappearing beneath a crest. It was a ballet, but with a partner more magnificent than any man. Stripped of my own romantic outlet as the years went on, I began to project all of my desires onto the ocean and its movements. I feared it so because I wanted it.

As a child, in those short winter months when the ocean was too cold, Zelda got her exercise by screaming throughout the house, pointing to where she believed we were being haunted—not just by the dead but also by events she claimed had happened in our own lives, only some of which we ourselves remembered. *That's the ghost of where I licked my most favorite ice cream before going to the fairy ball with Mommy in the ocean. Here is the ghost of where Mommy was sitting when she was wearing that pretty blue dress with the polka dots at the mayor's birthday party and then his mean son dropped his glass on the ground and started screaming at Ethel.* Perhaps this childhood fixation of hers is not so unlike the activity that most occupies my days now. I, too, hallucinate the resurgence of an ever-receding past.

Zelda's ghosts also assumed a standard human form: There was the mysterious woman who wandered up and down the beach, always carrying her red picnic basket and umbrella. In our bedroom lay a sick old woman with blue-stained teeth. And there was the butterfly woman Zelda chatted with in the kitchen, in various made-up languages, the woman who breathed beautiful moth-shaped flames. She was the one, said Zelda, who had burned down the house—the house that stood right *in this very spot, Mommy*—after the cruel boy chased her so hard through the woods that her baby came out of her dead.

It was only in the old shed, where Zelda always found shelter during a game of hide-and-seek, that she identified a ghost I shuddered to recognize. *He's tall and freckled and really tan and has got a hoarse, deep voice. And he's always asking for you . . .*

THE PHONE RINGING THROUGHOUT the house disperses our ghosts to half a century in the past. "It's for me," Zelda shouts.

To spite her, I pick up the line in the bedroom, hardly breathing. At last our roles have reversed. I am her naughty child.

"Gordon's in the hospital again," Zelda says. "So I'm here for a few weeks. Apparently the cocaine, the gambling, the booze—they all feed the manic depression. Or maybe it's the other way around. You don't have to say it. I already know you told me so."

"Don't blame yourself," the voice on the other end replies. "It's not your fault. Look at your mother. So many of us marry our fathers, but you, you married your mother. Those types are good at fooling us. Beautiful. Generous. Charming. But then the façade comes crashing down and what are you left with? Your father spent a fortune trying to get Elle help just like you're doing now. And, my dear, I hate to say it, but none of it ever worked."

"I have always appreciated your candor, Deborah," Zelda says sincerely. "Send my best to Joe. I've got to get going, though. Have to make sure these two haven't slit their wrists yet."

"We hate that we've cut Simon off, Zelda, really we do. But we did all we could for him down there. It's been money down the drain, to be perfectly frank. I know he must feel sore. But now with Joe's medical bills, and this recall lawsuit that we're unhappily bearing, the burden—"

"Deborah, Mother's calling for me!" Zelda cuts in. "Love you!"

Zelda glides up the stairs and comes into my room, smiling as if the prince of Monaco has just asked for her hand.

"Who called for you?" I ask her, staring at the window, trying to look as sick as I ever have, and as sad.

"Colleague from work," she replies. She makes herself appear wholly occupied by reorganizing the exquisitely organized pillows on the window seat.

"What is your employment these days?" I ask. Zelda ignores me. Aggravation swallows her face. To think I suffered her in my womb for nine months, nourished her at my breast for nine more, and granted her every wish for all the rest of the days she has lived. "Have you given up on having a child?"

"Why do you always want answers to the obvious, Elle?" Zelda snaps.

"Zelda, I was waiting for a call," I say to her. "Please do not pick it up first the next time it rings. This is still my house."

Her face breaks before me. She weeps for a good long minute, her mask decomposing like those modernist portraits so popular when I was young. For a moment I see my child in one of the fragments, my ghost-hunting rascal again. She walks toward me, throws herself over my lap weakly. "You're still my mother," she cries. "Aren't you?"

THE SKY HAS CHANGED. All the desperate critters of the woods call for one another. It is growing dark. My daughter is thin in my arms, like feathers. A spiderweb of violet light spreads through the trees. I lean toward the window. There must be a party out there. Shimmering bodies. Glasses tinkling, laughter. A woman singing a low, sad song. I have always loved the anonymity of a dark and crowded gathering. As if I could wander in any direction, into anyone's arms. There will be a day, not so long from now, when there will be no more parties. Everything ends in the room of memory.

"Elle?" Zelda asks.

"Who's there?" I ask.

"Mother, it's me," she says, leading me away from the window. "It's time for supper."

A certain Raymond has joined us. Rather than make a mistake by greeting him improperly, I ask Zelda to go into the fridge and find me some mint sauce for the lamb. She looks at me with exasperation. I almost feel sorry for her; I never had to watch my mother's brain rot. I never even had to truly know my mother.

"There isn't any mint jelly, Elle," she announces. The house is slowly emptying itself of the things I love. I long to miss dinner, to walk outside among the trees, which are all alive with wind. The ocean must be doing something out there, brewing storms, ghosts of things that have happened here and will return no more.

"Where is your husband?" I ask Zelda. She looks at Simon, then at Raymond, incensed.

"Why won't anyone answer my questions today? You know I was expecting a call from my daughter."

Simon passes the butter to Zelda. "Elle, your daughter is right here."

"I know she is." My voice rises to a pitch I hardly recognize. "That's what I meant. Has your husband left you?" I ask Zelda.

"What did Deb have to say about Joe sending a check?" Raymond interrupts us.

"I didn't get a chance to ask," Zelda replies. "You know how Deb just bombards you."

"Clarke Junior said he'd get us a loan," Raymond says, turning to Simon.

"You and that Clarke boy, Ray. Did he ask you for your right testicle in exchange?" Simon asks.

"I am trying to talk to my daughter about what's happening in her marriage," I shout at them.

"Just because you're sick doesn't mean you get to be abusive!" Zelda screams at me, then leaves the table.

I have a thought that perhaps I am dreaming. I look at Simon's face, his eyes, his lips, his cheeks, which I have looked on all these years, and suddenly have the sensation that this is not my husband at all. That he is a stranger. Isn't it the case that a beloved usually wears not their own but a stranger's face in a dream? In dreams I know my daughter is my daughter, even if she favors Ethel. We revive the past and intersperse it with the impossible future. What has been and what will be collide. Time does not move forward, but falls backward.

Raymond's face is suddenly before me, leading me away from the dining room. His irises are so blue, blue as the Atlantic, so blue I question again whether I am dreaming—and now Simon wears Raymond's face. "Tonight, Ma, you get to have supper in bed," he says.

But sleep never comes for me. Once the entire house passes into a snoring chorus, I go into the garden. At this late hour, a blue shimmer branches out from the trees and through the atmosphere, drawing roads between what was hitherto invisible. I feel the desire of the stars, distant traffic lights reaching across their great highways of black. The wind is terrific from the ocean. A silent orchestra plays. *C'est une chanson* . . . An airplane passes through the night, and all of its trembling souls stare down at me. I cover my eyes and I am with them, thirty thousand feet in the air, my head on Simon's shoulder, bound for Paris. Zelda in my lap, still a baby, her face tortured by the engine's sound. Trees were a comfort, rain. The breeze and the sun. Space would tear us apart. The clouds were lavender below us, a blanket, unbroken. But I saw no ancient palaces or golden spears or angels' wings. Wasn't that the location of heaven? No, life has only this planet, pitted on the edge of nothingness. Home is nowhere else.

Paris is lost. I cannot see it, though I longed for it so many years after that brief visit. A memory remains: drowsy from the difference in hours across the ocean, sauntering along a cobblestone street, an old man and his canvas, dusk falling, the city impossibly brighter by night, the pirouette of French all around us, a bum wandering by, singing. Love was everywhere, unhidden. We walked hand in hand, Simon and I, but we were not looking for each other. The sky was different, closer, hovering just above the buildings, then suddenly aflame. All of Paris came into the streets, aghast. We were witnessing the end: the war had returned. But then a wise man hushed the crowd. "Aurores Boréales," he said, pointing to the light.

II.

Y'all get that lightning down here like we did yesterday evening?" Ethel asks. We sit before the ocean, watching a helpless fisherman casting his line over and over but catching nothing at all. There is no breeze off the water, no relief from the midsummer sun.

"It lit the sky up like an amethyst," Ethel continues. "My Elijah, he used to love them storms. He used to like fishin' for nothing, too, like that poor dope out there. I always felt like telling him about something better to do." She chuckles. "Like, I need my nails fixed, my dishes washed, my hair done. But Elijah, he always put the ocean ahead of me."

"Ethel, have I—" I say, then stop.

"What, honey?" she asks.

"Have I always been sad like this?"

"You poor thing, don't you know it yourself?" Ethel asks. "You were happy, too, or at least you pretended good. You used to throw such nice parties. They all envied you, Clarke's wife and her gang, even though they acted so gosh-darn smiley. Sometimes I reckon they cast a kinda evil eye on you. And then that fellow of yours started haunting you again. Gabriel. It ain't my business if he was really your cousin. I can't blame you for loving a ghost so hard, what with Simon and his business and all those . . . those *associates*, as Elijah called them, always coming around," Ethel says. "Then, later on, it was just doctors, all of them hovering all over you. That's when you got *sad* sad, like everyone talks about. They just don't have a good memory. Hardly anyone is good at really remembering how things was. Except me. Elijah used to say I got the memory of an elephant."

I look down at the sand and see Gabriel's shirt lying in it. The one with the hole in the armpit. The one he always wore, that he wore that last night. The sun glimmers on the sea, preparing to set, and there he is, staring me down, gulping me back through time.

"Hell, I'm not any better than you," Ethel goes on. "No matter how many times I seen it, when I look at the ocean, I just see my husband's face. I still think sometimes he'll come walking out of it. He loved me, sure, but the Atlantic, her right here, was his great love. He found his life's calling on that ship—on the *Blue Rose*. Even he couldn't believe a colored man could love a job and get a pretty check for it, too. All the other jobs he came home cursing. Oh baby, he was always sayin', the plantation never died, just came back reincarnated. But the *Blue Rose*, he called that ship his baby grand. Sure, sometimes he had to mouth off Mr. Simon for treating him, well, you know it, Elle, like the *associates*. But he was real happy all those years. 'I'm just out there playing my music, baby,' he always said. And he always came home to me.

"But then one day Mr. Simon called everyone around." She coughed. "Decided there was gonna be no more jewel hunting. The company was gonna make that snake medicine instead. They didn't need Elijah's eyes onboard, so he could run on back to keeping the grounds . . . and there went his sweet song." Ethel limps down toward the water. "Sometimes, I can't figure why that broke his heart more than everything else that happened. But sometimes I can."

At twilight, I open my eyes. Ethel is no longer talking but beside me asleep. The ocean sings to itself beyond us. The fisherman has retired for the night. A trace of whiskey floats off Ethel's breath. She snores and her head falls lower and lower down her chest, until eventually it rests on my own shoulder. A sudden vision of Lyra. A ghost town. Wild horses strolling down Main Street. *Everything on the island is closing, isn't it?* But that is the future. Somewhere in the past, Ethel's husband died on his boat, two miles offshore. One gunshot to the head.

That morning, Ethel did not come to work. We had not heard the news, and I remained in the kitchen all through the day, waiting for her figure to cross the yard in one of her polka-dot dresses, a bright silk scarf on her head.

Days afterward, I found Ethel on the beach, sitting in one of these same chairs. It was that morning I first noticed the trace of whiskey coming off her breath, bright and early as it was.

"What is the date today, Ethel?" I ask below my breath, mostly to myself. Something important happened, she told me, on this particular day. How is it that my knowledge of it is already gone? But that memory of only hours earlier has slipped off the deck of this sinking ship. Once, I suffered recurring nightmares of the *Titanic*, but only now have I begun to envision its underwater afterlife, its deluged memory, the sea moss wrapped around its banisters, handwritten letters bleeding out, read only by the sea. All the ocean is a haunted house.

I shake Ethel awake. She opens her eyes like a child, slowly and adorably, perturbed to find it is already night.

"What's today again, Ethel?" I ask her.

"Oh, you're a real tearjerker, Elle. I told you, it's the day I lost Elijah all them years ago." Ethel shakes her head. "And you yourself was goin' on and on about him before. But things are gone just like that for you now, ain't they?"

The tide growls against the coast. One last pony gallops past us, kicking up the sand, running for home. The cicadas are up, crying against the dark, reminding us there is an end to this world. Ethel stands up and dusts off the sand from her dress. "I'd better get you to the house. I promised Mr. Raymond we'd be back a long time ago."

"Y'all look sea-kissed," says a young man in a sugary drawl when we approach him in the driveway.

"Mr. Raymond," Ethel says. "I tried to get her back earlier, but she insisted like she does."

"How do you do?" I say, not wishing to upset whatever is our relation. Inland from the sea, the clouds rest heavy on the trees. The sky will just coddle us until we can no longer breathe. Raymond lowers a box out from his truck and I see it is full of stacks of paper. His arms are strong and youthful, but his gut is distended. A thin sheen of sweat covers him. He's got a boy's head of hair, brilliant and black atop his skull. But it is his eyes that arrest me, so beautiful, so blue.

"Feel better?" He asks me as if my well-being and his existence were deeply entwined.

"She's all right," Ethel says on my behalf.

Raymond doesn't quite look at me but just past my shoulder, hiding from me whatever inclination, whatever disappointment, has passed over his face. "When I'm done here, can I trouble you for one of your famous lemonades, Ms. Ethel? I'll give you a ride home afterward."

"I can walk just fine. Don't need you driving into a tree again on account of my lemonades," she replies. "Wish I'd whipped you when I found you in my sauce in the first place."

"Oh, Ms. Ethel, I woulda gotten into somebody else's eventually," Raymond replies.

After the two of them exhaust their foolish exchange about a simple concoction, I ask the man at last why he has come. "Are you meeting with Simon?"

Raymond shakes his head and looks away, then covers his face with his hands. He appears to be weeping. "It's like she blames me for being here. For finding her on the beach that morning."

"Oh, shush up about that now. She's sick, Ray. You don't wanna hear the damnable things she says to me. She'll be all yours again tomorrow, you'll see. She always trots off to Shangri-La by nightfall. Here's a hanky," Ethel says, embracing him. "I'll leave you a sip of lemonade. Our secret between you, me, and the Lord."

"What are all these boxes?" I ask him once she's left us.

"All my paperwork," he replies, barely audibly. "I've got to go through every page of the accounting for the last fifteen years so I can show Dad over a whiskey dinner exactly how it was me, not him, that ruined everything."

"Good heavens," I say. "Have you been fired?"

"It's worse than that. We're bankrupt. And everyone's abandoned us. Even the Clarkes."

"Well, this entire island is employed by my husband. Perhaps Simon can help you in some way. That is why you are here, no?"

"Your Simon is out driving all over the state of Georgia, bleeding the rest of what we have on medicine men and quacks," Raymond says.

"Why would he do that?" I ask. "Is he sick?"

"He's convinced there is a cure for what you have. He blames himself. Even before the recall, he . . . He loves you so very much, you know," Raymond concludes.

"What are you really doing with Simon?" I ask. My hands begin to shake. I have never said anything so bold. There were so many men through the years, so many boys, but I never said anything. I never met one face-to-face. One who pretended to be my friend this way.

His eyes grow wet again as he draws up another cigarette. "You know me. I'm your Raymond."

"I don't believe I know you, sir," I say. "I am very sorry."

The young man collapses on his pile of boxes and draws the handkerchief to his face again. "You remember we had those parties out on the beach every Fourth, Ma? You'd stand at the grill with Dad, from morning until night, cooking dogs for every kid on the island. We'd beg you to take a break and you'd shove us all off, telling everyone it was your son's birthday party, and this was your gift to him. You always gave me your birthday, even though mine was a week later. I was the luckiest boy in the whole world. What other kid got fireworks for their birthday? And you always danced with me, every birthday, until I got to be a teenager. I know I told you it was embarrassing, that I didn't want to dance with you anymore. I'm sorry for that—I hate myself for that now. Don't you remember any of all that, Ma?"

12.

Simon walks to the window, opens it, and draws a long breath. From his pocket he unfolds a magazine. "Twenty years gone in an afternoon," he whispers to the oblivious night. "Thomas Green the geologist sent me a letter with this poem earmarked in this old *New Yorker.* He says I loved it ages ago, but I hardly recognize it now. . . ."

Simon pats the window seat beside him, then reconsiders and finds me in our bed. He handles the magazine's pages as if he were caressing butterfly wings. When I am very close to him, I rediscover his handsomeness, my own husband of all these years, the princely cheekbones, that sweep of hair, once black, now white, across his head, the prettiness of his plum lips, and the long lashes covering those famous blue eyes. And it has not just been his face and clothing that are so beautiful, but the way he has moved through life, deliberate as a dancer, equally elegant while eating or holding a magazine, as he is now. Simon has always known all the gorgeous rules. His hands fall over the paper; they have grown paler, I see, and sadder. Entropy is undoing Simon's ability to maintain them. "You remember him?" he asks, finally opening it to the page where the poem is printed. "The gentleman from New Orleans?"

I don't remind my husband that there were always two such gentlemen: my Gabriel and this Thomas, his Thomas. I conjure the face of Thomas's wife, Genevieve. "When was it he left Lyra, again?"

"The late sixties, I think. Went back to Louisiana. Or was it the seventies? Whenever we transitioned to the Caeruleum. Thomas was such a romantic when it came to those jewels. He didn't want any part of . . ." Simon drifts, then regathers his composure. "Well, he's living alone in Savannah now. I was very fond of him, as you may recall. As I was saying, he left because he did not want to become involved in the new pharmaceutical arrangement. I suppose, in the end, he was right."

I wonder at the implications of his living alone—whether Genevieve has already passed—but refrain from probing further. If encouraged, Simon will collapse into a maudlin reverie of the good ol' days with his dear Thomas, which can consume an entire evening. "Simon, I can't read this poem he's sent you without my glasses."

"But you don't wear glasses, Elle," he says.

I have always worn glasses for reading; now I reach pathetically for them from the table on his side of the bed, if only to win this pathetic battle over the state of my sanity. "Perhaps you forgot that I've worn them for decades because you are always stealing them from me," I say.

Dissolving our little spat, Simon reads the poem aloud, *and twenty years gone in an afternoon*, past me to the empty house, the silent rooms, the den and its dusted billiard table, the sleeping garden, on through the woods, all the way out to the murmuring sea.

"I recall now why I liked this poem. It reminded me of the beach house at Neponsit. That line about the sun and the shutters and June. We always arrived there in June," Simon says, once finished. "Remember?"

"I wouldn't know. I was never there, Simon," I reply.

"You were there, Elle," Simon says. "I know it. We spoke about it before we were wed. When we were still in the city. And then I brought you there. . . ."

So long ago, when we were still only engaged—October, November, far past the season for trips to the sea—I asked Simon to describe to me the house in Neponsit, his favorite place in all the world. I was trying to disrupt another of his many spells of silence. His face brightened toward me when I said *Neponsit*, as if its mere mention had rained new and beautiful clothing on my figure.

"Ours is the last of them all, at the very end of a row of houses! And you walk onto the balcony and there is nothing at all, just blue and more blue. But the most magical part is that, on the other side of this tiny strip of land, if you squint your eyes, you can see the Empire State Building!" Simon said to me.

Back then, I tried to smell it in advance, the Neponsit house, its linens of perfumed salt. I imagined rubbing my face against them like an eager and hungry cat. Not only would he take me the following summer, he went on to say, but one day it would be ours.

But there is another reason I remember that day so vividly: it was the day that Gabriel and Simon first met.

In Simon's sudden excitement for me—or, perhaps, for his longed-for Neponsit—he had insisted on joining the driver to escort me home rather than sending me home on my own, as I had always gone before. Shame passed venomously through me. I did not want Simon to see where we lived. It was such an entirely different world from his, where music floated out of seven-bedroom apartments. We lived in two different versions of New York that should never have mixed. The driver seemed to know his way around my neighborhood; I wondered if he lived near me, if he traveled, as I did, between two realms. I felt sure that Simon would quit the engagement then and there, but he seemed to look upon it all—at the street vendors' carts and the shouting and the smoke, and the masses of people, all the general ugliness that plagues the life of the poor—with the same tranquility as when he had gazed out over the river earlier that afternoon, a melody forming in his head about it. Or perhaps he wasn't seeing anything at all. Perhaps he was still caught in his trance—a child building sandcastles on the shores of near or far Neponsit.

When we arrived, Simon lifted me out of the car, more affectionately than he ever had—a princess from her carriage—and guided me around the puddles in the street. I looked up, and from nowhere there was Gabriel. For a moment he appeared to me as he must have to the rest of the world: A man without a home, without a single article of clothing that was not ripped or stained. A man who had not bathed in days. A man no woman with any sense would marry. He appeared shrunken and emaciated, as if the world had grown too large and full of possibility, of fairy-tale beach houses, for Gabriel to remain in it.

I squeezed Simon's hand and said it was already very late and that I had better run upstairs on my own. Gabriel shouted my name accusatorily, but Simon never reacted. "Next summer in Neponsit, my dear," he said to me in parting, oblivious to his foe. To Simon, Gabriel was of no consequence. He was a mere detail in the landscape, a faint apparition, as the poor always are to the rich.

"No, I was never in Neponsit," I say into the dark. Simon is gone. The wind has lifted the aged magazine from the bed, its pages now splayed open to an advertisement for Camel cigarettes. Nothing else from that past remains: not the Neponsit house, not Gabriel, hardly my husband or me. I want it all back. I want a hot dog from Coney Island. I want to look in the mirror and find my body shining, blemishes of youth across the chin and cheeks. I want to be haunted by the music of sex in the bath, before bed. I want to smoke and to drink and to make love and to smoke again. I want to want. But time has no further reservations with desire for me. Life diminishes our breadth until we are but the size of a grave, and then less than that. I shake Mina, to get her to look at me, but her tired eyes just blink flirtatiously and then close. I cannot tell if we are deep in summer or already in fall. The fog presses against the windows, making the island as gauzy as the blind dream. Perhaps the seasons are on the brink of ending completely to make way for a fifth time of year, one when the sky and the sea no longer have a barrier.

Since no one is here to mind my coming or going, I leave for a walk. There is no moon. Indeed, it is like that fifth season, the one that will draw the next world into our own. There is lightning in the clouds, a bonfire gathering in the heavens. When I am halfway across the lawn, the house disappears completely.

I rest in the beach chair. The sound of the sea draws me into the diaphanous world of sleep, then back to the long drive before our home—but at the door, inviting me in, are two old ladies I have never seen before. Inside, the house is in a marvelous state of disrepair. The staircases slump, the fixtures droop from the ceiling; the lights in the chandeliers are either dimmed or fully blown out. Dust clings to everything. The house is stripped of furniture, except for a single room I have never seen before, furnished with nothing but a bed I am informed will be my own. The ladies say: *We are happy you are here. Welcome, welcome.* I glance out of one of the windows and expect to find the ocean again but instead the oak trees are afire. Their branches grow flames rather than leaves. Black smoke subsumes the sky. When the ladies notice my eyes wandering out onto the destruction, they draw close to me and ceremoniously shut the blinds.

"Where am I?" I ask them.

"You have always lived here," they say.

Dawn rises over the sea. The last streaks of night and its parade of stars fade in the west. Day emerges again in gratitude to the killing hand of time. All possible shades of pink and purple reflect off the water. I look back at the woods with the fear of my dream, that everything is on fire, but instead of fire I see again that blue voltage shimmering through the branches, traveling into the sky, pulsing and luminescent. Then, walking along the coast, beneath umbrellas of a very different era, are the two ladies from my dream. They pause before me and look up at me in the chair. One carries a red picnic basket. For a second, I stare across the sand at myself. Then at Ethel. I close my eyes again, and open them, and two wild horses have taken our place.

I quit the scene fast as an old lady can, not quite running, but not walking, either. Back in our driveway, I am relieved that our house remains. Simon and Raymond are in the car. "Where have you been?" Simon screams when he sees me. Looking down, I realize I am still in a nightgown.

I hunt quickly for a proper-sounding excuse. "I was walking to Tilly's," I say. "After I lost my glasses, you see, I . . . And I was thinking about Neponsit, so the ocean—"

"Tilly's is gone, Elle. It's been gone for many, many years." Simon looks at Raymond meaningfully.

"I know that," I say with a shudder. I knew it was gone. I just wanted to see what it had become. "I had this dream . . ." I start to say. I have to tell them, to warn them. "Our house is being haunted—Simon, you know this. By the ghosts of those who want to burn it down."

"We're not doing this with you today," Simon says. "Get in the car. We're already late."

13.

The trees speak in that language granted to them by the wind, bending and lashing and shivering. We drive through their branches into town, disrupting their dialogue. Everything appears to be closed, even Leroy's Diner. Zelda would always order three pancakes there and drive me mad by eating only one. Simon's breakfast was three eggs sunny side up and sausage gravy and potatoes with toast and jelly, the rest of Zelda's pancakes, and a coffee or a cola, and never once did he gain a pound. I restricted myself to a grapefruit and a hard-boiled egg. Ridiculous now to think of all those wasted weekend brunches of denied pleasure. All the onion rings I might have consumed, all the fatty bacon, the luscious corn muffins and buttery biscuits. Leroy's windows are shuttered now; one solitary man appears to be living, or dying, on its front bench.

Two people shuffle outside the church, passing a brown bag between them. Curses I shall not repeat are scrawled on Tilly's shop walls. The contents of a compromised trash can fall out unapologetically. Windows are shattered in all the old storefronts. The town that was is now a fading postcard stored only in my mind. It once took patience to drive down Main Street as people criss-crossed the road without care. Now even their ghosts are gone. Their faces return for just an instant as we pass, shards of some minor exchange—the grocer tossing leeks into their containers—*My blessings to Mr. Simon*—the taste of rainbow sprinkles as the ice cream shop cashier bade me farewell—*I hope it's to your liking, Mrs. Ranier.* We were all, for a time, living inside the same dream of a place. We could not know how beautiful everything really was—until now, when Lyra's emptiness is the only breath that haunts the thin yellow steel of the car.

"Simon?" I venture.

"Yes, dear?" he replies warily. It is likely he has already explained all this to me—why sand has filled the doorway of the pharmacy, why an oak branch has split the candy shop in two.

Before I can muster some clever way to inquire further, the town is quickly past us and we are merging onto a bridge I don't recognize. I clutch the car seat. The way to the mainland was always by ferry, dolphins chasing alongside, then that moment when, 'round the river bend, Lyra vanished behind us. I used to fear that moment, its reminder that the bodies I loved most in this life were too easily disappeared by water.

Even once I can no longer remember my own name, I will still have memorized the trail of freckles that graced Gabriel's torso, the way his hands were sculpted, encompassing the whole of mine in his twice over. I can still feel his lips against mine, feathery and tentative. I loved to press against the skin of his belly, the muscles beneath well formed but not garishly so. Some days he was Irish, some days French; he was the son of a Gypsy, or perhaps a Spanish king. Even Gabriel did not know. The only sure thing is that I'll never get his body back—that body I loved to watch move across the earth, that body born in the streets beneath the constellation of Cygnus, so he always said. *Where the dead go out and the born come in . . .*

"Elle!" Simon shouts. "What were you trying to ask me?"

"Where are we going?" I ask.

"The doctor," he says, turning to me. "We just spoke about it. We're going to the doctor."

"Do you know the date today, Elle?" someone asks me. I find that we are no longer in the car but in a room tortured by light.

"August," I say aloud.

"August what?" the man asks.

His line of questioning summons that August back in the fifties, when a hurricane sucked the water so far back from the shore that the sea itself disappeared. We walked out to where, days previous, it licked our feet and found a blank canvas—seashells, dead seaweed. All the water in the world had been ripped off the face of the earth. But even in that desert I could not find Gabriel.

"Yes. It is August," I repeat.

"Do you know the year?" the man asks.

I review the decades. The thirties were New York, the threat of rain, of starvation, of war, of an ending; the forties we arrived on Lyra, dressed in pearls, a shimmer, we were alive when so many of our young were dead; our children were children in the fifties and there were so many children everywhere for whom we grilled and the smell of meat and charcoal carries me back to the ocean on some bright Sunday in July; it was in the sixties I began to feel so alone, the war was close, all over the television, closer than the moon, and my children were no longer children. I returned to New York at last, horrified that time had reached 1970 and beyond. And then there is nothing. Where was the rest of my life?

"Nineteen seventy-seven—" I reply.

"Not quite. It's 1998, Mrs. Ranier," the man says. "And do you remember me? I'm Dr.—?"

"I'm Elle Bell," I interrupt the doctor. "You must be thinking of some other patient. My name is Elle Bell."

The doctor looks away from me to Simon, nods his head, and makes a note with his pen. I hit the desk very strongly. I want the desk to break. I want the building to fall into the sea. But nothing happens, so I beg the doctor to please turn down the lights in his office.

We leave after that and Raymond drives us in silence. The August heat recasts the world in a yellow haze.

The first sight of Lyra always catches my breath, that lonely strip of land lurking off the coast of Georgia, mighty enough to face the Atlantic, hushed beneath its haunted oak. There is a secret stored in it that, after all these years, I still want to know. Then there it is, our house, its widow's walk peeking out from the woods. I see someone walking upon it, young, her hair catching the wind. She takes flight.

"Why did you say your name was Bell?" Simon asks me.

Where do you even come from, Gabriel?

Cygnus, I told you.

What happened to New Orleans?

I'm not from anywhere in this burning world.

But what is your family name?

Elle, you ever notice how the gods don't have last names? It's just Zeus, Poseidon, Cronus.

Everyone has one.

Okay, then make one up for me, Elle.

How about . . . how about Bell? Gabriel Bell.

"I've been married to you all these years. Has that not been enough?" I reply to Simon.

Simon hits the dashboard, then opens the car door and slams it behind him, leaving me with Raymond.

"Want a cigarette, Ma?" Raymond asks. He lights his own and regards the smoke affectionately.

"You resemble my father," I say to the boy.

"You always say that," Raymond says. He pulls a flask from his jacket pocket and drinks from it quickly, then sighs. "Wish you at least had a photo of him."

"You really do," I insist, but evening has fallen and I am too fatigued to pursue the topic. I step out of the car and make my way out into the garden, my cigarette preserved. I am shrunken again to the size of a little girl walking beneath the tangled oak. And then I hear the ocean. The night has risen above it, clear and profound. I know that once there were only stars, distant but still bright over the sea. Here on this island, with so little electricity, we could trace patterns of our own making between them. But the blue light now colonizes the sky, drawing star lanes between stars I've never seen before, unveiling before me the truest constellations. Cygnus rises on the horizon. Nebulae drip from the distances into my hands. This night knows no such thing as black; it is brighter than day.

14.

We strolled through our city at the blue hour, as the evening lights ascended over the rivers and across the bridges, darkening only upon reaching the sleeping land that was everywhere beyond New York. By then the technology of light was a familiar miracle to my generation, yet I still felt awe at the jewelry that dressed Manhattan at night. I wanted to be a woman just like my city, gleaming.

But there was an invention even more gleaming than light in our day—the cinema. One afternoon, back in time, as I shuffled through the masses gathered on the city's roasting new asphalt, New York was suffocated by a storm that refused to fall. Gabriel had promised me a ticket to see *Gone with the Wind* at the Loew's, where he had gained temporary employment. But when I arrived, he produced something else from his pocket: a pair of train tickets.

"What about the picture?" I asked him. "I've been dying to see it all year."

"Too hot for a picture," Gabriel replied.

"Did you get fired again?" I asked. His inability to keep a job was so persistent, I wondered whether he'd ever worked at the Loew's at all.

"I've just had a better idea," Gabriel replied. "We're going to a pool party."

"Those stolen?" I asked, as he fanned himself with the tickets.

"Borrowed," he said.

Half an hour later we were in Pennsylvania Station, running for a train to take us out of the hot city and into the greenness of everywhere else I had never seen. I pressed my face against the half-open train window, and as the wind blew fresh upon us, smelling of pasture and the sea, I wondered why no one had ever bothered to explain to me how beautiful it was just outside of New York.

"Here!" Gabriel cried suddenly, pulling me out of the compartment and onto the empty platform of a seemingly abandoned town.

"Where are we?" I asked.

"A magical kingdom called Long Island," Gabriel replied, sipping from his flask of whiskey in broad daylight like a regular lush.

"How is it you know anyone here?" I asked him.

"I don't," Gabriel replied.

"Well, how are you taking me to a pool party then, Gabriel?"

"Oh, it's simple. An old trick I learned when I was a child down in New Orleans. On a hot day like this, you walk around a fancy neighborhood until you see where all the fanciest cars are parked, and you just use your sniffer to find your way to the house where the swimming party is. Then you go right in through the front, like you're one of them; if they ask who you are, make up an extraordinary name and you say, ever so modestly, you're just in town to give an interview about a picture you recently starred in. And if one of them wants to act like some kind of expert on Hollywood, you can always say you're a French actor in town from gay ol' Paree."

I threw up my arms in exasperation. "You are absolutely mad! Movie stars dressed like us?"

"Look!" he said, pointing. On the very block we'd wandered onto, a crowd of cars was lining up beside a gaggle of men in white suits.

Gabriel licked his hands and pressed down his hair, then fixed my own curls, tucking a few strays behind my ears. As we approached the valet, Gabriel's entire gait changed. He stood taller and wider.

"But where is your vehicle, sir?" a young man asked, nervous at being suddenly put in such a position of authority.

"Oh, but don't you recognize me?" Gabriel faked a British accent. "I live just over yonder." He pointed vaguely across a field. "Walking is good for the constitution, I daresay." This was good enough for the boy, who, without further question, granted us entrance.

"What did I tell you, Elle?" Gabriel winked.

The house, if there was one, was shrouded by a forest of trees, too exotic to be indigenous to New York. I looked up toward the sky and saw only a green and glorious arboretum. We made our way down a cobblestone path that wound around fountains and patches of sea-blue hydrangeas and rosebushes, roses that must have been splendid in another season but now had browned from the heat. Gabriel peered into a smoky-looking blossom. "See how the spider mites have made a ghost of this rose."

I had never seen such a thing before, that wraithlike shroud smothering my favorite flower. But I would see it again, later, here in my own garden. And it was then, examining the death of all those roses, that I spotted the house we'd come for at last.

It was not a house at all, really, but a château with vines clambering up its front, and floor upon floor of cloistered rooms behind curtained windows hiding the promise of chandeliers. The lawn was decked with lanterns and candles and waiters passing drinks. And beyond it a pool that still sparkles in my mind, as long as a city block and full of the most gorgeous people I'd ever seen. All the world could marvel at the luster of New York, but this spectacle was reserved for the special few. At that moment, I wanted this life for my own; I never believed it would one day be mine—or that I'd be happier in the wanting than in the having it.

"Elle, can you speak in the good French, like they taught you in school? My Cajun won't do. And I'll be the Englishman," Gabriel said. "We'll pretend we're actors from Europe, and we're here for a . . ." He paused, hunting for the perfect image, then drifted off without finding it.

All that day, we brought the silver screen to Long Island. Gabriel was a British gentleman named George and I his French mistress, Isabelle, and because we were very interesting on account of our backgrounds and his charm, we were given swimming clothes after George explained that in France we bathed exclusively in the nude. As Isabelle, I entered a pool for the very first time. Gabriel guided my body as we moved up and down the length of it. I had no need to swim; I was weightless in his arms. We were movie stars, defying gravity.

We drank drinks of so many colors, I can still taste them distinctly: bright red with Campari, later minty with absinthe, as the host tried to impress us with his collection of liquor from the Old World. We stayed through the evening, eating the cheese and the fruit and the delicious smoked meats, and a young gentleman with a high-pitched voice gave us a tour of the grounds, the rose garden and the statues and the ponds and the tennis courts. Later, inside, he directed us to a piano that belonged to an apparently very famous man. The shoreline was just there, the young man said, nodding through the trees. "If you listen carefully, you can hear the Sound," he whispered. We obliged this moment of silence, though whatever waves might have reached us were drowned out by the decadent roar of the party.

And then suddenly, as if some silent alarm had rung, we were the last people there. Gabriel ambled toward me with that broad stride of his, a stride made for riding horses across deserts; he lifted me in his arms and ran us up the drive, out the gate—dropping his accent to howl at the valets for letting a pack of regular gypsies in, that we'd made off with all the jewels and, impossibly, the famous piano. One valet, the oldest among them, chased us until he collapsed into a fit of coughing, which painfully reminded me of my father. And then we were back at the station, dripping drunk, crawling into our seats, without tickets, without a penny, on the last train for New York.

"George, je t'aime. Je t'aime," I said as Gabriel collapsed on my shoulder, his mouth lolling wide as if he were ingesting all the stars and planets. "Isabelle," he said. "I love you, too." We confessed our love not to each other, but to whom we wished we might become.

And then, for no discernible reason, I desecrated our most romantic hour. "Gabriel, I'm engaged. The ring, the coat . . . I lied. They are all gifts from my, well, fiancé."

Gabriel looked at me imploringly, scanning my face for some sign of retraction, that what I had said could be unsaid. "You're not supposed to break my heart tonight, Isabelle," he said finally. "We're still starring in the movie."

"But we aren't in the movies. And my father lost his job. There isn't enough money, you see."

"There's never enough money," Gabriel replied.

Then we were silent for a very long time. Our bodies fell away from each other. How painful that is, that pitiful moment when two animals in love feel the emptiness of air between them return. Out the train window, I watched the moon pass below the black line of trees.

Gabriel smoked for the rest of the ride. When one cigarette had finished, he lit another, and so on, as the buildings of New York rose densely around us. When he spoke again at last, his soliloquy was directed less to me than out the window to the city itself. "I'm gonna invent something. Something more splendid than electricity. Better than even the cinema. I'll dress you in jewels. That's what every woman wants, right? Just because I wasn't raised with money doesn't mean I don't know how to get it. I'm an American, after all, Elle. It's in my blood."

15.

Many summers later, I returned to New York by train—this time as a wealthy woman, with Simon beside me across all that empty, painless air. We had taken the Palmetto from Savannah, then sauntered across Pennsylvania Station, with a man beside us to haul our bags and to find our taxi, saving us from that which bodily differentiates the rich from the poor: exertion. Still, neither the years nor our money had fixed the sweltering weather.

We stayed at The Plaza, taking turns in the cold shower before appearing for brunch with Joseph, whom we'd seen only a few times in the decades since his visit to Lyra. Unlike Simon, Joseph had grown less handsome with time: he had lost much of his hair, and his youthful muscle had devolved into extra weight, making him all the more uncomfortable in the heat. He spent half an hour with us, fanning himself miserably, all the while hunting for sport among the exotic ladies who seemingly had business at the hotel. Unaware of his brother's distractions, Simon was working anxiously to convince Joseph of something: *additional investment*, yes, *the equipment we need,* from somewhere far away . . .

"But you've gotten nowhere with this scheme, in all this time, Simon. How long have you been digging in those waters? Thirty years?"

"That's because we didn't have the drills to go deep enough. The real stuff, I'm convinced, is out farther, and what we're pulling up is just residue drifting with the currents. These new drills are revolutionary. No one in the history of mining has ever done this, Joe. This isn't like oil." Simon was pleading now. "We're like the first men to walk in space. We're trying to discover something that no man has ever held in his hands. These stones hold the secrets of—"

"This isn't like walking in space. In space there are planets and moons. Down there, so far, it's zilch," Joseph replied. "Besides, they just found diamonds in the ocean off Africa. Father sent you to the wrong coast. Personally, I think he got fed a tall tale by that good ol' boy Clarke. Next, they'll find diamonds in the North Pole and we'll still be digging around in a humid swamp. We're not even in the game anymore, Simon."

"But," Simon began to protest, "this is my project. Father assigned it to me and not you for a reason. He told me—"

"You're right, and the good news is, despite your own thickheadedness, you've come across something that might be more lucrative than we expected. My Yale boy—and I know how you love those Ivy Leaguers—has been studying that dust from the phantom jewels you sent up our way. He says there's some medicinal use for it. We don't need the darn gems whole at all!"

"Have you lost your goddamn mind, Joe?" Simon's voice shook.

"Everyone here in New York says the future's in pharmaceuticals. Specifically, for psychiatric treatment. Goddamn happy pills. Diamonds are the past. Who needs a diamond when you can swallow something that makes you *feel* like you're made of money?"

"You can't actually believe that the Caeruleum residue can be used for a useless pill!" Simon shouted.

"What the hell was that, Simon? Celery-*what*?" Joseph asked.

"It's Latin for 'blue.' My trademark for the gem," Simon said proudly. His gaze wandered dreamily out of the room, the way it used to at the piano. "It has the flair of the classical. I can see the ads already: 'Eternal Caeruleum.'"

"You better leave the ads to us up in New York. Eternal Celery is no 'A diamond is forever.'" They bickered some more, but the die was cast. "This is the last check I'm signing for your little folly," Joseph announced, his eye resting on a redhead perched by the elevators, a younger, curvier doppelgänger of Deborah. She returned his gaze. Later, they would doubtless have an appointment.

"And one more thing—about all those people you're still carrying on your payroll," Joseph said. "Do you think your little sandcastle really requires hundreds of workers?"

"Mining is not easy work," Simon insisted, descending from his recent blue-toned vision.

"All right, little brother. Enough interrogation. I'm starting to sound like our mother. Come out to Southampton this Friday, pay us a visit. I'll get you the money by then. Besides, it's always ten degrees cooler out there, I swear it." Joseph stood up to leave, peering toward the lobby to ensure that the primary conquest of the brunch had not abandoned him.

"Southampton? What happened to Neponsit?" Simon asked, bewildered.

"Ah, we sold that years ago. Too much riffraff. I forgot to tell you—I've been dabbling a bit in real estate as well. You'd do well to diversify yourself, Simon—but I know you're a romantic. Making money for money's sake is for us vultures."

As it was fated, we went to Long Island the following Friday, driving out of the humid, summer-sickened city into the fresh, green sleeping world beyond. From the window I hunted, the entire way, for that château beyond the trees I'd been to decades before. It was near dusk as we approached the valet in Southampton, and I looked on in wonder at the line of stunning cars before us. *One day we'll drive cars more beautiful than these*, Gabriel had said, his arm locked in mine, as we shuffled toward that nervous valet all those years ago.

Joseph and Deborah's home sat on four odd acres, edged against a colder, more apathetic Atlantic Ocean. The walls were all perfectly white, the surfaces too clean, and a pot of orchids set at the square center of every table. The hedges were trimmed all along the yard. There was nothing wild left. Even the ocean beyond the estate was disappointing, its view displayed there for all time with no oak or dune to veil it. The help attended to us from the service entrance, serving us tiny flecks of pastry with names they could hardly pronounce. The party, instead of beneath the twilight, was held stuffily in a tent. The crowd could not stop guffawing over the attending musician; I heard the ladies whispering that he was a great genius, a graduate of Juilliard, a soloist about to tour the globe. "He belongs in a department store," Simon said of the pianist, jealously though astutely.

Deborah, in a gaudy perfume, searched the scene for her husband like a panicky pigeon. Finally, her eyes landed on me, her lonesome sister-in-law. "Elle, you must try one of these vodka martinis. They are more slimming than wine, and far more fun. Wine just makes you *depressed*," she said as if following a train of thought.

"Oh, are martinis all the rage in New York this month?" I said, feeling suddenly that I'd never been a New Yorker at all. New York was a truth beyond question only to those locked inside of it. "Well, call me old-fashioned, but I still prefer wine."

"Oh, Elle, you're adorable. At least we know Ray got his voracity for liquor from the Raniers and not you." She chuckled, then turned her gaze beyond me to more interesting company.

Could this be the same magical Long Island I remembered? Joseph's was the sort of party that makes life feel irreal. Beneath the chattering faces I saw cackling skeletons. As Simon passed from person to person in the tent, I sat nursing one glass of wine, then another. These people, I sensed, knew something about Simon that he himself couldn't know—the way they smiled at him, once he spoke his name, nodding with familiarity, then made their apologies a dozen seconds too soon for polite disregard. Simon no longer belonged to New York. This society was for those whose money could never disappear. And ours had as a foundation only a phantom treasure.

At last Simon surrendered, returning to me.

"All these Yankees can go to hell," he groused.

"Oh, and I suppose you're a real Confederate now?" I said.

He looked at me more darkly than I had expected. "Did you speak to anyone at all tonight?" he asked. "You could try, Elle. See how these wives all wear their pearls *and* make conversation, too? They're intellectuals." He emphasized this last word like I didn't know what it meant. "Down in Lyra, you used to be the life of the party. I don't know what's happened to you—"

"Time, Simon," I replied. "Time's happened to me, and to you."

We emerged from the party early, back on the path toward the valet by nine in the evening. There was nothing above us, no tree shroud or mystical rosebush, nothing to shelter us from the oblivious New York sky. Simon hailed a blank-faced valet, a professional, not a boy blinking from fear.

"Excuse me, but aren't you Mr. Ranier's brother?" the valet asked.

"Fuck Mr. Ranier," Simon muttered.

Without missing a beat, the valet removed an envelope from his shirt pocket. "Mr. Ranier entrusted me with this envelope for you. He told me to tell you it's for that celery you two spoke about."

RETURNING TO THE CITY—to that bestial August when the country was still at war in Vietnam—we spent our last day shopping along Fifth Avenue. How much did we spend? It didn't matter to Simon. He had Joseph's check in his breast pocket, and he still believed we were soon to uncover the wildest of fortunes, one that would finally be wholly our own. The crowd down the avenue moved slowly, pausing every few steps to stand in awe of the fashions in the shop windows.

"When we get those gems out from under that ridge, Joseph won't know what hit him," Simon went on, as if to himself—a sermon on blue and diamonds, starlight, star bright, completely unmindful of the human traffic swarming around us. It was too hot to jostle or push or walk any faster than everyone already was, so when the shirtless man approached us, we had no way to avoid him. His face came so close to mine, it seemed he might kiss me. And then, as soon as he passed, I found my purse was gone.

The country was full of men lately returned from the war, looking shaken and confused, and this one seemed to fit the part. His pants were ripped, his hair disheveled. Strangest of all, he didn't run away; he seemed to have no intention of actually stealing my purse, only taking it and tossing it back and forth in his grimy hands. I felt, as I've often felt with the mad, that he was the recipient of some profound truth I would never know. "I can smell you, you know," he shouted in a broken voice. "You think you can smell me. But I can smell you. You stink just like me! *You stink!*"

With that he threw my purse into the street, and all the contents poured forth from it. As we scrambled to draw up the strewn items, he jumped into the screaming crowd, disappearing and reappearing to me among their faces. "You all stink. The whole American soil stinks," he yelled. "You know what you stink of? You stink like money. Money stinks worse than the shit out of your ass. Try and smell it. Put that dollar bill up your nose and see you don't smell the scent of your own putrid souls."

I could still hear his voice once we were safely inside The Plaza, cosseted by the lyrics of "Autumn in New York," sung by a woman in a dazzling gold gown. I smelled something sour in the subtle perfume wafting through the lobby, there to invoke the impression of money itself and all it could buy: the illusions of safety, security, beauty, immortality. But money has only ever been that—a prosthetic, a mirage. It never did save my life.

"Elle, you're shaking," Simon said in the elevator up to our room. "You know, maybe Joe is onto something about these happy pills. What if we mentioned them next time we pay a visit to Madera? It couldn't hurt if you tried something new. They seem to be very trendy here in New York."

16.

Further back in time, to 1961. "We're off to see the wizard!" Simon said on the drive to my first appointment with Dr. Madera, who was fresh out of Harvard at thirty years old. I would be his first patient in Savannah.

But the story doesn't begin there. Where does it begin? Sadness is a wave. It had been coming for me a great many years. And then suddenly I was beneath it.

Let's say the wave found me at the same time as Genevieve, whose husband was the geologist hired and loved by Simon to prospect on our ship, on the *Blue Rose*. Thomas and Genevieve, transplants from Louisiana. She was originally from Paris, it was said, a bit of je ne sais quoi Thomas had picked up after the war. Lyra's streets were perfumed as she passed through, by both her cologne and the steady stream of cigarettes attached to her pretty, painted mouth. The two had no children, which made a couple strange in my day. From the instant I saw her, I wanted to know her. And then one day there she was, lingering on the street outside the bank, offering me a drag from her cigarette, her voice husky and only slightly accented, though her syntax gave her French origins away. "We both look like we could profit from more fun," she said. "This is what is wrong with us."

She was a handsome woman, not quite of our time, not quite of the past or future, either. Her eyes were so dark blue they were almost black, her cheekbones severe, and with the exception of her lavish bosom and long, wavy chestnut hair, she might almost be mistaken for a very beautiful man. She looked at you like a man might. Devouring.

In the blurry moments that ensued, I found myself accompanying her to Grey's Tavern, where I had never once been a patron in nearly twenty years living on the island. Once inside, alone with Genevieve and the bartender in that room that stank of sweat and booze, I didn't protest as she ordered me a Scotch and herself another, and another, and then another.

After half an hour of nervous introductory banter, Genevieve interrupted to say that she'd never enjoyed this sort of conversation. This was revolutionary for the time; petty conversation was what women did together. Instead, she asked bluntly: "Do you love truly your husband?"

"Why, yes," I replied automatically.

Genevieve chuckled, but her eyes settled on me as if she'd seen something tragic.

"What's wrong?" I asked.

"Rien," she said. "Only our husbands spend *much*, much time together, you know?"

"Well, they work together," I insisted. "On the ship. Close quarters make fast friendships."

"Tell me, did you ever love another?" she asked, following a reverie of her own. "I had a lover when I was a girl and I think of that lover every day. We always had music together. Do you know that feeling? Like there is an orchestre symphonique when you embrace?" She was slurring almost romantically now, as if she were singing lyrics to me. "But then my lover was married off to a man. It was like she died. And so I married, too."

I looked away anxiously and noticed we were suddenly alone. "The garçon has left us here," Genevieve said. "You see," she then pronounced very soberly, "I know all about your husband, because I know the truth about mine." Genevieve did not wait for me to respond. She took her hand and placed it on the thin skin of my pantyhose.

"What do you want?" I asked, my insides shivering.

"I want to try with you what they do every night to each other," Genevieve said, her mouth already upon me. "Have you ever kissed a woman before?"

She had taken nearly all of me when three men, one of whom was Clarke Junior, stumbled into the bar. They were already descending upon us when the Clarke boy slurred: *Well, whaddya know? The fairy princes have got dykes for wives.* I ran from the bar, face covered in my hands, into the empty nighttime streets.

For months I waited for the gossip to crash down all over my marriage, but it never happened. Perhaps those boys were too blind drunk for the events of that night to survive in their memory. Still, I could not get my hands clean enough. I wanted Genevieve, wished her to do what she had done and more, but when the desire snaked through me, I found something sharp to quiet it. A razor to my thigh, a knife to my fingertip. In the mirror, I looked at myself and found my body everywhere bruised and bloody. But Genevieve haunted me still, the smell of smoke in her hair. It was as if she had brought Gabriel back. I became convinced it was his ghost in her body, calling for me. Finally coming back for me. That she was his wave.

Out on the beach one night, a perfect piece of driftwood had washed ashore. I took it in my hands and beat myself with it, there at the very center of myself, until I could feel nothing but a deep, blissful, burning pain. At last I was only light, disappearing through stars. I would see Gabriel soon. But in the morning, a young boy found me on the shore, bleeding, shivering, whispering to myself. My body had not left me; it smothered me still. I asked the boy to abandon me there, but his hands dug deeper around my chest, clutching my hair. His young eyes were swollen with tears. Raymond, my Raymond.

After I was released from the hospital, Simon drove me to that first appointment with Madera.

Dr. Madera was so young then, with a complexion that would make him seem young forever. A blond wife. Educated at Harvard. For someone I saw so often, whom I've met more times than I ever met Gabriel, that is all I have ever known about him.

At that first appointment, Madera weighed me, took my blood pressure, checked my temperature. I thought he might invite me to recline on a couch and reveal the content of my dreams, my secret obsession with my father and hatred of my mother. But none of that, Madera announced, was relevant any longer. At five feet nine, I was down to 110 pounds. "How's her appetite?" Madera asked.

"She hardly eats," Simon replied. "But it's just a little illness, like you said, right, Doc? Almost like a cold?"

"That is my belief, despite what others contend," Madera replied. "That diseases of the mind cannot be distinguished from diseases of the body."

Simon trusted wholeheartedly in the medical sciences—it is where all the dust of his phantom gems went, after all. If only we'd been born one hundred years later, Simon would have found a way not to die. Then again, if we'd been born a hundred years later, I would never have had to marry Simon. I would be living on one of Jupiter's moons with Gabriel.

"Nevertheless, I'll have to ask her some questions directly, to see how serious the illness has implanted," Madera replied to Simon, as if I were my husband's dog. "Mrs. Ranier, how often do you have thoughts of death? Did you mean to hurt yourself on the beach? Do you fantasize about harming others? Do you have suicidal ideations? How often do you feel happy? How often sad?"

I had *wanted* to lie on the couch and talk about my dreams. I had *wanted* to tell this nice young man how often I still dreamed of Gabriel returning, as if from a foreign land. To tell him how, though I was so happy to see Gabriel, there was always something off about his appearance: He would seem suddenly old or too young, or thin, so thin I thought he might die all over again of hunger. He was poor as a beggar and as dirty. Or he would appear as someone else entirely, talk from beneath someone else's face. Occasionally and only very briefly he would appear as he was; his dream hands would reach for me, try to draw me close, but before we could embrace, he would slip away, disappear in a dream wind. I wanted to ask the doctor why the living dream so vividly of the dead—but just as I opened my mouth Madera shouted my name, less like a doctor and more like a drill sergeant. "Return to this room, Mrs. Ranier!"

I stared out the window, seeking the deep azure of the Atlantic, longing for its waves to return me to their womb instead. "I just want to go back . . ." I began to say aloud.

"Mr. Ranier, I would not recommend psychotherapy or hypnosis. These are outdated, unscientific methods that are not going to work on your wife," Madera announced without further inquiry. "But I can offer her electroshock treatment, which has been utterly groundbreaking."

I FLOATED HOME TO Lyra after that first appointment. There was no car, no road, no journey; no time seemed to pass between sitting for the sentence enacted upon me by those electrodes in Madera's office and reclining with Simon in the garden hours or days later over Ethel's egg sandwiches, my hair caressed by the wind.

"Simon," I said, "Lyra looks like it's been painted with blue all through it."

Ethel peered around nervously. "Where you seeing blue?"

"Lightning bugs," I replied. "But blue."

Simon had already picked up his newspapers. That day, the first human being, a cosmonaut, was sent into space. "It will get better, darling. Look, you're even eating your lunch."

What could I do but wander away from him? I set out on the road north, the branches low overhead. It was wilder there, the soil smelled better. Fairies flitted around me, flickers of light gallivanting between the trees. This land was unmarred by human want, immune to Simon, to Madera. I could almost hear that man up there, all alone, so many miles from Earth, crying for home in my mother's native Russian. I crawled into the cradle of an oak limb and became a part of the tree, my skin changing to bark, my hair to moss. My veins were shining, incandescent. Lightning danced on the edge of all things. Opposite me I saw Genevieve, lying naked in the tree.

"Do you feel happier?" Simon shook my arm, interrupting my

daydream. The sky was closing in on me again. Where had my private wilderness gone?

"I feel so happy. You can't imagine how happy I feel," I replied steadily. "I think I'm all better now."

"Good, then we'll go see Madera again next week. He says consistency is important."

17.

Late summer. Overnight, our retreating star has sapped the green from the trees. A hurricane ravages the water fifty miles offshore. These are my favorite days, these maudlin Sundays, when everyone else has gone away, left me alone, and the water roars against the gray coast, the wind mighty and melancholic enough to herald the return of a more beautiful God. Every piece of metal and glass and silver on the island clangs and chimes to the storm, and all the bells in the distant churches ring a new music into the world. And I am returned to Simon's home on Riverside Drive some sixty years ago, where we sat over supper in our last days in New York, the only sound that of the maid replacing our salad dishes with supper dishes, *clang*, *clink*, and then on to cheese and dessert. And when everyone else had placed their utensils at the proper diagonal, *clink, clang*, to summon the maid again, mine remained on either side of my half-full plate. The maid stood to my side, so nervous I could nearly hear her heart beating, until Simon announced: "Miss Cumberland is finished."

From that day forward Simon would announce when I was through with a meal, even long after I had gained my awareness of the protocols of china and silverware. And didn't that summarize, in three simple words, what it is for a woman to grow old? *She is finished.*

I never adapted to the art of drinking to blur the violence of such thoughts, to arrest the march of memory, or to dissipate the angst over the ending of one's time on this planet. That escape was Simon's. Nightly he returned home after emptying a bottle of bourbon with the help of whomever, *an associate*, and proceeded to drink another bottle of wine with dinner. Never did he yell or hit me. He was more or less a happy drunk and spoke mostly aloud to himself, his soliloquies a mix—depending on how much he had imbibed—of forgotten piano melodies and digressive tangents on the ongoing hunt for the bluest diamond. I sat with him for hours in the evenings, watching him grow messier, more hysterical, pretending to listen, a stale glass of water at my side—until one day when, for no particular reason at all, I decided it was time to get dead drunk and have it out.

We were, by this time, middle-aged already. The children were grown enough to look after themselves. It was a fifty-degree day in December, and we were down on the beach, four bottles in. The skies were cloudy, but we'd protected ourselves from any chill with wine. Chatting about nothing for hours. Gossip, really. The men who worked for Simon supplied an endless amount. Then, suddenly: "Are you angry with me?" Simon asked. "Is that why we're here? Why we're drinking?"

I had no reason to be upset with him, I replied. Unless he knew of one himself?

"Because I've betrayed you," Simon confessed at last, and he began weeping then, and because of that, and perhaps because daylight still reigned implausibly overhead, though it felt so deep in the night, I started tearing up, too. But why? Truly I no longer even knew. I cried often in that time. I woke up to it; it was my certain weather. It was that inescapable. The wave would never pass me by.

"If I just could figure out the melody," Simon said, diverting from his admission of betrayal. "You see the jewels glowing, just three feet below the surface, they tug at the drills, heavy as lead, and then—they're out of the water for one second and . . . and then, *poof*, they're gone."

"Gone? I don't understand," I replied.

"To *dust*, Elle. They turn to dust as soon as they leave the water. Like a melody, there and gone. We've been trying for years, but we haven't found the way around it yet. Even Clarke pulled out of the company. He's the one who sold us this goddamn delusion in the first place." Simon began to slur. "And I don't know how long we can keep the employees . . ." He paused, distracted. "And, yes, I've betrayed you. I've betrayed you badly. Over and over again."

I could barely follow Simon's drunken thread. We were both smoking then, Simon and I—everyone was smoking then—and I remember our lanterns along the beach had just flickered on, and their light was so gauzy beneath the fog of our cigarettes that I wanted to lose myself there, to wander into some realm less defined, less oppressive, than the one Simon had brought descending on our own.

"Do you know why they banished me here, Elle? Because they found me with Elgan, the piano teacher, the famous one, the one who was going to make me famous." Simon fumbled to open yet another bottle, dripping wine into the sand. "I was going to play Carnegie Hall and the London Symphony and I'd be the king of goddamn bohemian Paris and I was going to be famous famous, but then they saw me with him—oh, they wanted me to be like Joseph, be like good Joseph, so well adjusted, but I wasn't like Joseph, I was in love with Elgan, so they rushed to have me married to the closest . . . *heh*," he murmured, trailing off.

Who really wants to hear the truth? The full truth. To press him further was like sniffing at a dead corpse, but I couldn't resist. "Closest what, Simon?" I asked.

"My father saw us and we were only holding hands, innocent as two schoolboys, and he screamed at Elgan to get out—'Get out, Elgan, get out, you faggot,' he said—and Elgan ran right out and he didn't look back and I was thinking all the while, *David*—that was his name—*David, save me*, but he kept on running, and the next morning Father told me he was going to find me an appropriate marriage. But just in case I was an embarrassment, it would have to be to someone outside their circle. So Father decided on this little worker of his, someone who worshipped him, the one who had a pretty daughter, but far outside of his society, so the gossip could be contained. But that wasn't enough. The pretty, poor daughter and the faggot son had to get engaged quickly so they could go far, far away, too far away for any future rumors to reach New York. But at least there would be jewels in exile. Shiny melodies, Elijah calls them. Elijah's about the only one who still believes in them."

When Simon finally finished, I began, against all reason, to laugh. I laughed so wildly that it verged into crying. Simon started laughing, too. We went on that way for hours, long after we finished the last bottle. In not belonging to each other, we had found a way to be together at last.

"And then there is Thomas." Here Simon drifted into a commotion of tears. "You know, my geologist on the *Blue Rose*. The one with the French wife who lives apart from him now . . . in New Orleans. You know, there has been Thomas—"

At last, I discovered why I had never once seen Genevieve again on Lyra after our encounter, though I had seen Thomas. One evening, he and Simon were very nearly camouflaged by the woods past the shed, wrapped into each other, as if mimicking the entangled oak branches. Simon appeared to me then as a complete stranger, a phantom, a trick of the dusk. I had missed my habitual attendance of the sunset, watching them from my hiding spot. And when the sun's abandonment turned the sky crepuscular, I heard

Simon laugh, truly giggle. I was almost happy for him, happy that the one he loved was abundantly present, whereas the one I loved was dead. But then Simon would go on to lose his love, too.

"Is the wine all gone?" I yelled that day. The alcohol had abandoned us, just as Genevieve had and Thomas would eventually. We were alone in our misery, as every couple has been since Adam and Eve. Simon fell fully into self-pity; he tore down the beach away from me, throwing off his clothing, howling like a madman as he jumped into the ocean. I closed my eyes and conjured a vision, of Gabriel returning from the water in Simon's stead. But this end to the story was in some ways sadder. Simon had become my best friend. I had spent most of my evenings on the planet listening to him at the piano, each note struck perfectly and mournfully, and heard in each melody that dream he had, of playing music halls and concert stages on Broadway, David Elgan applauding in the audience, rather than hunting dust off a forgotten island with me. In that moment, as he tore into the surf, his body disappearing and reappearing, pale and steadfast, I understood that I would be a ghost first, that I would die first and be the one to watch over him, an old man at the piano, forgetting his notes, trembling over what might have been.

"Yes, the wine is finished!" Simon yells back across the years. My vision clears. I am sober and withered, and in Simon's place at the shoreline is a familiar woman with long gray braids and a warm chestnut face. She beckons me toward her. The wind and rain are all over her, having their way with her skirt and billowing inside of her shirt. On the sand behind her sits a red picnic basket.

"Come on into the ocean, dear," she whispers, though yards away, now waist-deep in the sea. She holds an umbrella foolishly overhead, even though the water already has her entire body in its grip.

"It's time to come inside, Ma—storm is here," a man's voice calls from behind me. He takes my hand forcefully in his. His breath smells of lemon and the sharp hint of vodka. "Ethel made fried okra. Your favorite."

In the instant between beholding the man's face, his sad blue eyes, and returning my gaze to the ocean, I see that the stranger has already walked so far out that the waves have swallowed her neck. I struggle away from the man. I want to recover her. I scream for her, but a wall of rain rushes toward me. The body of the ocean yearns to just cover me. Soon it will cover the entire world.

Another figure emerges through the blinding weather, breathless. Simon has finally returned from his swim. But how has he already dressed? All the bottles on the beach from our afternoon together have vanished. What year is it? What day? My name is Elle. Elle Ranier, née Cumberland. The stranger has sunken into the waves.

"Ray, we've got to get inside!" Simon shouts. "It's really coming in!"

Raymond is before me again. Who is he and why is he here? He gathers me into his arms like I'm his child. Simon trails us. A creeping sensation grows in me, a feeling that perhaps this has happened before. That this is all that has happened. No other memories reign. We have been two miserable souls, acting one scene: Simon following miserably as I am taken away from the ocean and my desire to fall into it, thrashing and screaming. We are locked in these roles forever and ever. I wonder if this is how it ends, all of it.

Lightning coils in the clouds extravagantly above me, like a revel of snakes. I am stung. Blue unravels me. I look frantically back at the ocean. But the woman is gone.

"She was out here talking to some imaginary person. Like she used to after the electroshock," Raymond shouts. I writhe helplessly in his arms.

"Don't mention that word!" Simon screams at Raymond. "Or Madera. You know how she gets."

The days return, the weeks, the years, tumble down on me again with the rain, terrific and relentless. Madera's mouth. One, two, three. Elle, you ready? Blink. Ray, Simon, Ray, Simon. The clamps are cold. My mouth hurts. Shut your mouth. One bottle, two, three, Genevieve, I have to go. I can't see. I was just tired. I am just so tired. I have to go. The fifties, the sixties, the seventies. Just two pills, just three pills, just four. Make it five. One, two, three, *start*. A bathtub full of a drop of blood. Let's try something new, something blue. Yes, Joe, let's call it Caeruleum. You were right. You were right. It's working for Elle, it's really working! Zelda screams: It's ruining her, Daddy! She's not there! She's not even there. All that blue just yonder un bon marche chérie au ciel Elle Bell you and me a sweet reverie c'est une chanson I'll never forget. Ethel frowns oh now why'd they go and try to take all the blues away no no no the blues always come back Lord don't I know it.

The hurricane changes course and recoils from Lyra through a black stage door in the sky. Even the horses emerge from hiding to bid it farewell. Everything returns to life. The birds chat frivolously, as if spring and not fall were on the horizon. It is always after a deluge that we animals suffer the delusion of miracles. Our house reconfigures itself around me. I wish for once it might transform as it has in my dreams—grow extravagant hallways leading to secret, magical rooms, rooms decadent with velvet and gold, where fairies wander and cats talk and angels do govern the living, rooms I never realized were here, rooms I've fallen for again and again only to awaken and find them gone.

This house, in its true form, was a dream to me once. I was stupefied by its beauty. Like Simon's apartment on Riverside Drive, I believed our estate here on Lyra had sentience, that it watched me stumble down the stairs and trip over its humid carpets. I would never be elegant enough for it. Then one day there was nothing left to trip over, no spiderweb left to memorize. The house had become mine. I knew the feel of the silk in the beds on my skin, their scent, which blue china complemented the mahogany dining room. My hands grazed, day after day, the dusty spines of hundreds of books in the library, so many of which remained lonesome and unread. I could lose my hearing and still recall the music of the creaks in the stairs, the sighs of the ceiling, the ghost's cry in the first spit of water from the bath. I could lose my sense of smell and still conjure the house's perfume of tobacco, sandalwood, must, time, and rain. But all my magical rooms were in the past, and the future, for a long time now, has raced toward me like a lion hurtling toward my neck.

Still, Lyra, this buoy between me and the bottomless sea, has remained unknowable. The dunes of the island throw themselves against the ocean, keeping it in its place, but even they can last only so long. Soon wind will break the windows of this house. Soon these walls will crumble, and our home will burn into a circle of mysterious stones like the Clarke mansion before it. And soon this entire strip of land will be under the sea. Lyra will be a shipwreck.

For now, I go into the garden and raise my arms. The blue light rises from the ground, crisscrossing the oak like primordial snakes. I fall to my knees like the prophets before the face of God in all the forgotten deserts. The dead already move here. Their language is painted before me. Lyra disappears beneath such haunting illumination, as if it is already afire.

PART 3

Fall

18.

The sky and the sea are one again, as in the ancient days when the heavens had not yet separated from the face of the waters. All breathing on the planet has ceased. No horses aggravate the lawn. My Mina has disappeared. The birds have all gone, flown far away from this heavy atmosphere. I wonder if I am all alone, with only the company of weather—this fog that has re-formed the entire earth. For so long, I have prayed that just one thing in this life might attain permanence, even if it is this, this dominion of fog. But a human voice enters the room, and in an instant the climate is rearranged. "I'm late," he says.

"Late for what?" I ask.

"The meeting." He is no longer young, my husband, but remains thoroughly a gentleman in his becoming blue shirt, the color matching his eyes. "I've got to get down there. Ray's walking Clarke Junior over, and knowing Ray, before even saying *Hello, how are you*, he'll sell off all our jewels and our linens, too. I swear to God, that boy didn't get a single Ranier gene when it comes to negotiating money."

"What kind of meeting?" I ask.

He grows exasperated again. "Elle, I wrote it in your notepad in case you woke up and found me gone. You're having more trouble tracking these days."

"It must be the weather," I offer with a shrug, but my husband fails to nod in response. In my lap, I find a small leather-bound book. The pages are mostly blank, except the very first, where there is a little scrawl in familiar penmanship: *Clarke Junior's brought developers in again to discuss sale of the land. Holler for Ethel if you need something. Do not worry, my firefly. The house is ours forever. Love, S.*

"Love, S.," I say aloud.

"Oh! And, Elle, please remember not to come down to the office this time," S. says, rummaging in the closet before emerging triumphantly with a tie.

"Let me write that down for you, too," he says before kissing my cheek. His breath smells sour, age confused with peppermint. Cold sweat drips off his skin onto mine. I flinch as he draws up the pen and begins transcribing his note.

"It's the second time they've come, which means they're serious. Not the house, Elle, I know. I would never, as I promised. It's mostly the remaining Clarke land in the north and some of the property I bought in town. Clarke Junior'll back down on the rest."

"This house?" I ask, then look down at the book. *PLEASE*

STAY IN BED UNTIL I RETURN, a postscript to the original note now reads.

"Elle, dear, I'm sorry, but I really do need you to try to remember this. Last time you came down to the office raving about all kinds of island ghost stories and wildfires. These developers are very businesslike people. Clarke Junior says they're even interested in the Caeruleum site . . ." He trails off. "Well, I suppose they might find some better use for it than we did."

"Do you know if my father will be there, too? At the meeting?" I ask S. I feel as though I've been running through a forest that spans the circumference of the world, looking for my father, for a very long time.

My husband, in his pretty blue shirt, picks up a little mirror from the nightstand and holds it up to my face. Suddenly, I understand I have been dreaming the morning up—the godlike fog, the mysterious meeting, this S. moving around the room like a tired machine. "Elle, look at yourself. Look at me. It isn't 1939," he says.

But in my reflection is a woman whose irises are swallowed by their sockets. Blue medicinal powder is caked on her lips and teeth. Her hair is gray, falling out of her skull in two long braids. I have seen her before, sitting alone, watching me in the dark, from the beach, a shadow passing between the oak trees. The shivering begins in my fingertips, and grows more intense. I smash the mirror out of his hands and onto the floor. That will wake me up. Violence always ends these visions. I hit what remains of the mirror over and over against the nightstand until the woman fractures, disappears.

But the rest of the nightmare persists. S. shouts at me and I cover my ears.

"There was a woman here," I try to explain. "With blue all over her teeth."

Another figure enters the room and the fog evaporates all around her. Flames fly out of her hair. No, they are butterflies. "Thought you weren't giving her those pills no more, Mr. Simon?"

"Excuse me, Ethel, did you become a physician overnight?"

"I know what I seen all these years, Mr. Simon."

"Have you seen what I've seen, Ethel? Because what I've seen is a woman who has refused to leave the past behind for sixty years."

"With all due respect, Mr. Simon, I been here almost every day of those sixty years and I heard her tell you over and over she didn't want them pills, but you, being no different than most men, thought you knew better what was good for her."

"Can you tell me where my father is?" I ask them both.

When I last saw him, rain was falling over New York. It seemed the entire city lay sleeping beneath its gentle drum work, except for me. We slept on either side of a thin wall, my father in the living room on the sofa, me in the little bedroom beside it, and I fell asleep most nights to the soundtrack of his snoring. Sometimes his breath became caught in his throat, and in the sudden silence I feared it had stopped entirely, until a trumpet of sighs assured me that he was still with me in this world.

But that last night I lay on the mattress fully clothed and tip-toed into the living room once the snoring circus had begun. My father lay on his back, his face pale in the cool light from the street, his lips parted and bursting with broken sound. He looked defeated even in sleep, hands outstretched at his sides, supplicating to the God that had abandoned him so often. From his pockets, I delicately took two dollars for Gabriel; I had long since learned to steal without waking him. As I creaked open the door to the rest of my life, my father said something in his dreams—a few undetectable words, the last he would ever say—but I did not pause to try to hear them. That night, Gabriel was taking me to the Cotton Club.

Why is it that we never manage to still bliss? Is it because time escalates when we are happy—becomes as drunk and blurry as its passengers? Gabriel's sweat was my sweat that night as I fell into him and out of him, our hips tambourines, my shimmying feet detached from their limbs, dancing onstage after hours to the intoxicated saxophone. How did he know all these people? I wanted to know. I couldn't hear his answer, or my own voice; he kept walking away from me, his chest puffed out, impersonating someone or some instrument; he said something about Prohibition days, when there was money for people like him, and now there was nothing; they were pouring drinks from all sides into our mouths, a pretty face here, a prettier face there; Gabriel was talking to one and she kissed him on the mouth and I started to scream at him, at her; I was slapping him and he was laughing, pointing to the famous pianist, cigarette between his lips, conjuring a river of beauty; I thought we might dissolve into the walls and never get out and watch lovers for a hundred generations dance; but then it was morning and the bright rain was making its sad music on the concrete outside.

Back on Earth, my entire body shook with cold. I was wearing just a flimsy dress beneath a wet coat. I held my heels in my hands. All around us, men in suits rushed by responsibly to work, averting their gaze from our ruined figures. Hours had disappeared inside that club; there was no way to prove the night had ever happened.

"Too much to drink, Elle Bell. I'm taking you home," Gabriel said, as I began to weep. Something, somewhere, was deeply not right.

The journey downtown seemed to last for hours. The persistent rain had grown troubling, a clattering voice reminding us that every party ends. I knew what awaited me in advance; my body knew it before my mind did. I left Gabriel at the station and ran down my street and up the apartment stairs. It was too late. My father lay prostrate, just as I had left him, but he was no longer there. He would never be there again. *No no no no no no no no,* I cried, a whisper, then a wail. I did not stop until my voice gave out, along with my feet and my arms and my fingertips. It felt as though the earth might crack open beneath my weight. I pressed my face against my father's quiet chest and opened his hands, clutched tightly in rigor mortis around the few coins I'd left in his pocket—all that remained to us, to me. I threw them against the window; the metallic *jing jang* of their crash amid the rain commanded me to marry Simon. Money ruled life until death. Somewhere, in some time before time, men had made it that way. The realization was suddenly fact. I threw up in the sink. For the first time in my life, I felt I was made of flesh. There was no secret animus: I was of my father and mother, and to them, to dust, I would eventually return. That morning I saw my face old, saw it dying; life was on its way forward from that moment on. The former world had passed away.

The rain continued all that day and the next, until the day my father was interred, when it settled into a polite mist. Simon's father paid for the funeral, in a plot not far from the Raniers'. I wore a black dress of my mother's, one my father had brought out to show when he spoke of missing her. She was shorter than I; the dress settled just above my knees.

At the service, I was standing between Simon and his mother when Gabriel appeared, uninvited, wearing a midnight-blue suit that fell heartbreakingly well on his frame. He stood directly opposite me, the grave between us, watching me so intently, waiting for me to lift my gaze and return his. I began to weep then, though I also wanted to laugh hysterically. I could never look at Gabriel's face without smiling; even when he wasn't trying, there was always something of the clown in it. Suddenly, I felt punched by the dirt thrown over my father's casket. He won't be able to breathe! I wanted to shout. But I remained quiet. I have let everything I have loved be taken from me.

And then the service was over. Gabriel crept up behind me at the reception, whispering into my neck, the two of us gazing out at the long-dead fallen leaves, "Don't you recognize this place, Elle? It's our cemetery."

"Gabriel," I said with a sigh. "Why are you here?"

"Why am I here?" he scoffed. "Why wouldn't I be? You're my girl. Look here, Elle, I didn't want to speak too soon considering the circumstances, but—" He paused, looked around him. "The thing is, I've come into a very large sum of money. All I need to do is pay it back after a while, but it's ours, so don't you mind about that. So we can marry, and I can prove that I can take care of you. I *must* take care of you now. You don't need him, whoever *he* is," he whispered loudly. "I'm not sore at you, I promise. I've been irresponsible, I know. No kind of man asks the girl he's courting for money, even just the once because I was in an awful pinch all of a sudden."

"It wasn't just the once," I said.

"It wasn't?" Gabriel replied, looking truly bewildered.

"Who did you get the money from this time, Gabriel?" I asked.

"That's not for you to worry about, ma chérie," he said. "I spoke to Jerome—you know, the one in that business I told you about. You've met him—good guy, good family man, and he gave me a loan for a while to get us on our feet. Not for you to bat one beautiful lash about. Let's just go now. You just have to walk out of here. Tout simple. You haven't married anybody yet. It isn't a crime to change your mind. And now you don't even have to worry about what your daddy has to say."

I thought of my father's face there on the blue sofa, his broad, outstretched hands. What was he saying to me, those last few words mumbled between dreams? I thought of his sad shuffle, the way he always shut the door softly when he used to leave for work at six in the morning and return at six in the evening, and I counted in my head what I'd taken from him, one dollar here, five dollars there, though he never said a word in reprimand. I saw us at the sea when I was so very young, after Mother died, when Father brought me into the waves deeper and deeper and picked me up over them as I cackled and quaked in his arms. *Your mother is here,* he said. *She's always all around you now,* and that was when the ocean began to haunt me, and I screamed, because the ocean harbored ghosts, harbored death. Now my father, my first love, my only parent on this lonesome, whirling planet, was gone.

"But I promised my father I'd live for . . ." I began to say before being called away from Gabriel.

"AND NOW WE OWE some loan shark *half a million dollars,*" Zelda screams. Everything that was disintegrates with her piercing shriek—that long-vanished funeral, Gabriel's beautiful blue suit, his pleading, downcast gaze, that day we stood at a distance, formal as strangers. I stand, decades later, in my own driveway. Wild turkeys run gracelessly across the road. My daughter's pretty, forlorn face is smeared with mascara. I wonder again, as I have so often lately, how

I have arrived at this moment. It was only recently that Zelda was just a tadpole in my womb. Where have the years gone?

"Zelda, lower your voice," Raymond says, looking toward me. "She's been so good today. You're going to upset her again."

"Hey, Ray, how's AA going?" Zelda asks. "Because I can smell your breath from over here and I bet she can, too."

"That's enough. We don't have what we used to have, Zelda," Simon says. "I can't get you and that husband of yours out of this one, not this time. Have you at last given any thought to divorce?"

Beyond their voices I hear the sea settling into itself for the winter, its mournful singing through the trees a warning for the four of us. Zelda once listened earnestly to my tales of the mermaids, emerging from hibernation each autumn, their hair long and violet and shining. The jewels they wore, I told her, were the same ones her father sought. Nothing was fair, Zelda whined; why couldn't she ever see one while swimming in July? A valid complaint, I told her, but that's the way magic works. It's always just out of our reach.

"You have this house," Zelda spits back at Simon now, scattering her beloved mermaids to the world beyond. "You know Clarke Junior wants it. He's been groomed since birth to take back his daddy's old jungle kingdom, and now he can. Why not let the Clarkes take the fucking house?"

"We are not leaving the house," Simon replies firmly, then walks toward me and holds my hand. He squeezes it once, again, and looks at me with desperation. He wants me to say something, but all around us the branches are trembling as if something unknown is threatening to blow them away.

"What about all her bills?" Zelda flings her hands toward me like I'm already a corpse. "When will you just accept she's not getting better? Ray tells me you've been paying visits to every quack in the state, spending a fortune on potions and elixirs. Why not raise Edgar Cayce from the dead and ask him where we can find some rose water?"

"I never told you that!" Raymond shouts.

"Simon, I warned you twenty years ago you were poisoning her with your happy sappy Caeruleum. But now it's too late!" Zelda shrieks. "She doesn't even know who we are!"

I try to scream back that she is wrong. I built this dream. Simon. My son, my daughter, my daughter, my son. I carried them here, bled until they breathed. Zelda's first cry, that aching, ancient sound—I still hear it. I form the words in my mind, but I lose them as soon as my mouth opens, as if they were in another language.

"Where did Gordon even meet this loan shark? Or has he cuddled up with the Mafia again?" Simon yells, succumbing to the fray at last.

"The Mafia!" Zelda shouts hysterically. "The Mafia doesn't even exist anymore."

Simon's voice, once strong enough to command an actual ship, shakes unconvincingly now; it will never regain that command.

"You could have had *anyone*. We sent you off for a private education, which cost us a fortune, let me remind you. You could have found a lawyer, a doctor, a finance man, a man from a good family like yours. Instead you found some good-for-nothing from under a heap of trash in Atlanta who spends his time in casinos full of whores and squandering what little we have left on drugs and slot machines. Do you aim to destroy *everything*, Zelda? I suppose you share that instinct with your brother here, who worships Clarke Junior so much that he's invested our last penny in that crook's robot scheme. Not to mention handing him back *the entire goddamn island*."

"I am your daughter," Zelda says, between gritted teeth. "I am your flesh and blood. And this house is just a house that one day some hurricane will tear to the ground." She slams her car door and turns on the ignition. Simon's hand slips out of my own. His arms rise up helplessly. Raymond is weeping. Even the ocean roars. I cover my ears. There have been times in this life when I have been unable to bear the noise of the world.

"I promised your mother we'd grow old together here, and I'm not going to break that promise," Simon shouts at Zelda's car.

She stops, rolls down her window. "Let me use my Ivy League education to explain it to you. You wanna shit on Ray, but how about all that fancy mining equipment you spent a fortune on? Hunting some fucking myth sold to your daddy by old Clarke Senior—"

"Don't you get started on that!" Simon shouts.

"You know where Ray and I got our bad habits? It's you. Sure, I married a gambler, but then I had a gambler for a daddy, didn't I? At least Gordon has been after real money. My daddy wouldn't ever give up. But when his dreams finally turned to dust, he became a drug dealer to his own wife."

19.

It's your play," Ethel reminds me. I look to the plane above us for distraction from our card game. When I was very young, I imagined myself in old age surrounded by foreign artifacts and curios from travel, photographs amid the ruins of primeval cities. I believed I was meant for so much more. But these days I live now are the last evidence that I ever was, these memories of the end.

"You know, in this great big life, I never got to ride a single one of those," Ethel interjects, watching me watch the plane. "Seventy-five years on this earth and I've spent every one of my days in the state of Georgia."

"Where would you take that plane to if you could?" I ask her.

"Hmm," she replies. "I think I'd like to hitch me a ride to Phoenix, Arizona."

I try to imagine the place, dusty and parched beneath an imperious sun, so unlike verdant Lyra, nestled against all this blue.

"I saw a commercial about it just the other day," Ethel goes on. "The lady in it said it never rains there. Always warm, always blue skies. She looked happy. And ever since I was little, I had these returning dreams that I lived in the desert, and I'd ride across it on my horse, aiming at my enemies with my bow and arrow. I reckon maybe that was my past life."

"You really believe in all that?" I ask. "In past lives?"

"Oh, sure I do," Ethel replies. "I seen things and felt things about that. All the church folk pretend they only believe what they read in the Bible, even though they know better." She squints up at where the plane once was. Her eyes are turning blue with blindness. She follows its sound, though it has long disappeared from view. "I met Elijah before in another life. First time I saw him I knew it wasn't the first time, if you know what I'm sayin'."

Ethel lays down a quadruplet of hearts and then a double of sevens from my own stack of cards. "For such a smart girl, you sure give up easily," she announces of our gin rummy game. This produces no small amount of glee in her, despite the fact that she's been playing her own divided luck all afternoon.

"So where would you have that plane take you?" she asks.

"Across the ocean," I say.

"Across the ocean's not a very particular place, Ms. Elle."

"To Paris, then," I say. The yellow Seine sprawls out before me, flooding the stone embankments, dappled with light, carrying a song from bridge to bridge. No one there knew my name, where I'd come from. I could have so simply run away. The gray sky couldn't bear to be broken by the sun. Paris was composed by un dieu triste. The city held me. Longing had formed every alleyway; any café might harbor Gabriel, obscured by a newspaper, a cigarette in his hands, waiting for me to find him. *Isabelle, Isabelle.* The dead never die; they just wait for us to walk away from ourselves.

And then Paris is gone. I look askance at the coming night, splattered by the sad color of time.

"So why didn't you go on over to Paris in the first place?" Ethel asks. "Can't imagine you were taken prisoner down to Lyra."

Ethel returns to her impending, glorious gin rummy victory and I return to New York, to that luncheon one thousand years ago, as a snowstorm rolled up the Hudson, when Mr. Ranier first announced he had heard of a mysterious prospect on a tiny island off the coast of Georgia. I was still dressed in the black of mourning for my father. Just days or weeks had passed since I'd become an orphan. Mr. Ranier sat at the head of the table; Simon was at the other end, filling Joseph's conspicuous absence. The maid scurried around us, trying to achieve invisibility by being present all of the time, pouring us more water, the men more wine, slicing and serving us far more bread than was necessary. Simon's mother derived pleasure, at these lunches, from seeing the poor girl run ragged—deciding, at the last possible moment, that she required a particular sauce to be paired with the main dish before the meat was cool. On that day she demanded a mustard-shallot velouté, a recipe I hunted for for many years after that lunch but never uncovered.

The maid improvised as best she could, but Mrs. Ranier insisted it needed "more tarragon, more salt!" All the while, Simon's father was furiously criticizing the competition's saturation advertising. "Diamonds in every stinking daily," he griped. "Even with the war coming, they really think every Tom, Dick, and Harry is going to run out and buy a diamond for the girl next door before he marches off to die."

Outside the penthouse windows, the river was still drunk with sunlight. As we were waiting for the tea and dessert, Simon's father started raving about an undiscovered jewel, a blue sort of diamond, he'd caught wind of down south. "No, no, this is no diamond. Far more stunning than any diamond, I've been told!" He was wild-eyed with the idea. "The mother lode is still submerged, just offshore, but there's an island nearby. The perfect quest for a romantic man!" he shouted at his son.

As he spoke, I noticed that the light in the stone of my own engagement ring had suddenly disappeared. In the distance, through those same windows, the weather moved in a cavalcade of doom steadily north. Soon the storm would be over us, pounding into the roof, disappearing the river. The line between this life and the possibility of another had faded, just as my being there in Simon's grand dining room prevented my being beside Gabriel inside a rickety shed of cardboard. But Mr. Ranier paid no attention to the tempest, preoccupied by his tales of that beautiful island, *where property is a steal*, where Simon would put the family name back in the books for good.

"So why hasn't anyone else beaten us to it, if this site has what you say it has?" Simon interjected at last.

"Because no one else is a Ranier!" his father replied. "You know how you were raised: you can't be lazy when it comes to innovation. These gems can't be shoveled. They've got to be dug out from beneath a shelf in the sea."

"How am I supposed to get jewels out of the bottom of the ocean?" Simon pleaded. "Dive for them?"

"Well, you've always been *a good swimmer*!" his father said, roaring with laughter. But he was serious. "Quit your whining and think for a second. They drill oil out of the sand now. Why not jewels from the water?"

"Georgia is rather far away," Simon said quietly. "And what about my music . . . ?"

"We're talking about the future!" Simon's father interrupted, excited. "That's why we need you. I couldn't give this project to Joe. He's got to keep things steady, watch the numbers. You're the visionary, the creative one. Now you can put that musical . . . *nonsense* to some practical use."

The storm was entering its grand finale—a tremendous snow squall had replaced the rain, obscuring the remaining world—but neither Simon nor his father would quit talking. They were wholly transfixed, one by the prospect of money, the other by the pangs of familial betrayal. I shut my eyes, and in my mind's darkness I had a vision—an image of Gabriel, drowning in the middle of the ocean. But I was an unwise Cassandra, not yet able to interpret what I was seeing, that this image was a truth being presented across space and time. I opened my eyes, in shock, and dropped my cup of tea onto the hard wood of Simon's dining room floor. Out of instinct, I knelt down beside my seat to collect the shards of china. "Elle, stop that," Simon's mother said, slapping my shoulder. "That's her job." And indeed the maid was already there, by my side, with her little broom.

The squall passed southward and the sun reemerged, as if those fifteen minutes had been a kind of joke. "Well, like it or not, it's done," Simon's father announced, concluding the lunch. "The deal with my man in Georgia is in place. He's a Harvard man. Good stock. Name is Clarke. I'm sending you to paradise, Simon! You should be grateful. You've always loved the heat. Joseph and I will be stuck shoveling snow while you're sunning on the beach." Then he redirected his sermon to me. "And you, Elle Cumberland, you'll make a fine southern belle. . . ."

With that, we were dismissed. In the wake of the storm, I accompanied Simon on our customary stroll in the park. He walked with his hands behind his back, humming a dramatic melody, five steps ahead of me, swiftly and nervously. Almost jogging to keep up with him, I asked at last if he would like to discuss matters of the future with his fiancée.

"Georgia!" he cried. "Why not Hades? I don't know a soul there. I won't know anything about how to live there! How to talk to anyone, for that matter! They speak almost another language."

"I know someone who could help us down there," I blurted out foolishly. "He's a Southerner." If I could keep Gabriel close to us, I suddenly thought, I might save him from himself. "Won't we need a bit of help? Well, he's a jack-of-all-trades. And he's lived in New York, but he's from New Orleans, so he can help us settle in. He knows that world."

"And how do you know this someone from New Orleans?" Simon asked, a look of desperation in his eyes.

"Oh, he's my . . . cousin. Actually, you've met him, only you were never properly introduced. He was in the blue suit at my father's funeral," I barely stuttered. "And he's quite well spoken. You'll come to love him as much as I do."

A GUST OF WIND whips my last card from the table, flapping it in my face before it's carried out to sea. With her foot, Ethel captures the queen of diamonds in the sand. "Well, I suppose you don't need to tell me why y'all came. Mr. Simon must have heard that blue and shiny legend from old Clarke. He was luring folks into his nasty web in those days, after they got put out in the Depression. Not that Clarke was ever gonna stand by and let someone find blue here before one of his own did. That family's been down here hunting it since the first Fourth of July. Anyways, Mr. Simon got gems in his eyes. But when he dug, nothing came out. Elijah told him it wouldn't be easy as one, two, three. After all, Elijah'd been looking all his life, too, thinking he'd beat out the Clarkes, who owned his granddaddy and his granddaddy's granddaddy. Damn fool, my husband. Still, Elijah knew more than anybody else. But Mr. Simon was always so preoccupied by his associates. Especially that smarty-pants Thomas Green—if you know what I'm saying."

"Ethel, do you believe there's something down there?" I ask.

"I'm not saying I don't. But I sure didn't go blind from believing in it. Your Gabriel, he was too keen on it. Just like Elijah was. Guess we've got a type of man. That night you was married to Simon—I remember it well—Mr. Gabe skipped the fancy party and sat up all night with us in the guest cottage. I told him all the tales I knew. 'Course Elijah kept shushin' me 'cause didn't I know the treasure was his to find. But Gabriel kept poking around, looking for more, more, more. That's where money comes from in the first place, don't you think?"

Ethel waits a moment, then answers her own question. "That's right. The more stories there are about something, the more everyone wants a piece of it. That's how in the old times they decided what was going to be expensive and what wasn't. How many stories folks told about a thing."

20.

The day of my wedding. Springtime. A Renaissance painter had been revived to dramatize the secular April sky. I did not know what I wanted, for it to rain or for it not to rain. In my cream silk wedding gown, I walked through the bramble of palmettos. I wanted to bleed, though I knew no thorn could halt time.

Gabriel was standing on the beach, tiptoeing gently toward a wild horse, whispering to it in a language half human. We had been on Lyra for only a week. It still might have all been a dream. I touched his shoulder rather than say his name, for he was so close to petting the beast. No matter—it shrieked and ran from us.

"You know what I'll miss?" he said, without turning to me. A gray legion of clouds was marching in from the Atlantic. Suddenly, I longed for a monsoon. "I'll miss the snow. It doesn't just fall down, you know. It's not like the rain. It swims in the wind. Winter'll never come here. The seasons are why I went north in the first place. Down here, it's always just nice. Or hot. All the year round." Gabriel kicked a heap of sand into the air. "But we're just here for a little while. Like you promised. Enough time for you to get some money out of the divorce without it looking suspicious."

My throat choked. Mascara began to bleed down my cheeks and, without my noticing, onto my dress.

"The difference between you and me," Gabriel went on, "is that my heart is quiet. That's why that horse didn't run from me. Not till you showed up. My heart's not afraid. Is your heart quiet, sweet cousin?" He drew me to him and kissed my wet eyelashes.

I reached for him, wrapped my arms around his waist. I adored the hulk of him, the way he felt, like a statue of a man. "This was the biggest mistake," I said aloud, unsure whether I meant bringing Gabriel to Lyra or marrying Simon before the sun set later that day.

"So don't go through with it at all," Gabriel whispered into my ear. "You don't have to. That's the biggest secret they don't tell you when you're born. You can just say no."

My heart was not quiet. I could feel its violent drum work against Gabriel's chest. I shoved him off me suddenly, as if I were the terrified horse. He sighed and lit a cigarette. He was further away from me than he had ever been. "Go, then. I'll be the one who can't hold his peace."

"Don't hold it," I yelled, already running away from him.

Ethel was waiting for me at the edge of the garden, her hands pressed together anxiously as if she were my own parent marrying me off, though she was only a child herself.

"We'll need to fix that," she said, pointing to the black smear I hadn't noticed on my dress. Terror consumed me. I had never owned, let alone worn, something so expensive and in front of so many people. All concern for Gabriel and our tenuous plans for the future fell away. Propriety has been my Achilles' heel. Or perhaps propriety is a toxin of money; we become paralyzed by it.

"Baking soda," she said, seeing the look in my eye. She shuttled me off to the guest cottage and started working on the dress with a cloth. "It sure is nice you have your cousin working here with Mr. Simon," she said. "I can't imagine having none of my family around for my wedding day." She has always been good at filling the disquieting spaces with conversation.

"Sure is," I said, but I was shaking beneath her hands.

"Just nerves," she said. "I had 'em, too." We'd known each other only a handful of days, not long enough for me to know her intentions, whether she meant to spy on me or be my friend.

"When were you married?" I asked her.

"Three months ago." Ethel smiled. "Happiest day of this girl's life."

I glanced down at the dress; the stain was already fading. "You worked a miracle. Thank you," I said. "Will you be attending the party?"

"You're funny, Miss Elle," she said. "We stay back here in the guest cottage in case you need anything."

I blushed at already having given my naïveté away.

"That's all right," she said. "We have our fun. I reckon more fun. Now try and smile a little. You're about to be the richest girl on Lyra."

It never did rain. The night I married Simon there were billions of stars in the sky, and in the coming years, millions of people would be shaved and stripped and gassed, and men would unleash a nightmare by splitting an atom in two, and the soul of the world would be forever desecrated beneath that blast.

That day, Simon walked among our guests like a king. But the Clarkes were there shadowing him. They have always been lying in wait.

When Simon was not spinning me around and dipping me over to the romantic swing band gathered on the lawn, I sat alone at our two-person dining table, a frail speck. My flesh felt made of snow. There were stars and songs and laughter and the fizzle of champagne, platters of oysters and prawns, a feast of color and liquor, even fireworks in the end, but Gabriel never appeared. Gabriel had held his peace. I hunted all night for his face among the guests. I never stopped. The drunker I became, the more my propriety faded. I fantasized him coming for me, atop one of those wild white horses, and taking me away. But all that night he was hunkered down with the rest of the help in the guest cottage, sipping on a stolen bottle of Scotch, nourishing himself on the blue legend that would ultimately undo us all.

I awoke to the first pinch of sunlight on the horizon. Simon was asleep on the floor of our wedding chamber, still in his suit, snoring off the booze. I remained in my slip in our wide and unsullied bed.

From the window I heard the chatter of a few remaining guests, saying their farewells in the loud tenor of drunks. Among them was the booming, sonorous voice I later knew as Elijah's: "Now, Gabriel, don't you go out there hunting that blue and shiny! I know the ocean better than anyone on this island, and I been looking for it since I was a boy and still seen no sight of it. Just get your drunk self to bed!"

21.

In my wedding gown, I wander now through this city of oak. An incredible amount of time has passed. The woods have grown so dense, so tall, that their coiling branches occupy the entire sky. Blindly, through them, I reach the dunes. Everything is yellow. The beach smells of summer grass. Out to sea there are others, sitting in boats. They look at me impatiently, as if I have long delayed them. I walk toward the water, which is as clear as a pool, but endless. My feet shine below the surface. The sand is littered with objects that do not belong in the sea: watches, music boxes, my wedding bouquet. When I look up, I see a boat far from shore, my mother and my father upon it. I move toward them, but then the depth drops beneath me and I am already waist-deep. I try to make my way back to the beach, but I am restrained by a force in the water. I look back at the house. Its windows are shattered; its façade is blackened by fire.

The sun drops below the sea. A glow illuminates the water's depths, as though the moon no longer lives in the sky but in the ocean. The night is brighter than any night I have known. I go on. I pass so many boats occupied by strangers, until at last I reach the one that held my mother and father. When I get close, I find their faces obscured by blank space. I can see right through them, into the enchanted landscape beyond, and though I try to make my way back—

Raymond! someone screams from the shore.

I am inside the house. The mist is dense, pressed against the windows. I hear the scream again—*Raymond!*—as the first foghorns sound from the sea. A blue apparition passes through the trees, breathes against the glass, embracing the low clouds. It houses entire galaxies in its beating heart. We do not go toward the afterlife; it comes for us.

Raymond! Wake up! Simon runs through the yard and the blue recedes like a wave folding itself back into the sky. He runs toward the house, then back through the woods until I lose sight of his figure.

I skip down our stairway and leave the house in search of him. He must need my help. I want to run after him to prove I am still alive, to feel my lungs fill with air. Already into the woods, I remember I am wearing only my wedding dress, which is so thin, made for spring. The sunrise has not yet pierced the layer of oak. My bare feet begin to go numb in the cold, damp dirt. Where has the heat gone? The yellow sky? The oak are just shrubs. I had seen them so tall, so tall they reached the clouds. . . .

Simon approaches me breathlessly, puts his coat around me.

He draws me to the edge of the dunes. "Can't you see it, Elle? Do you see it, for the love of God?" He turns away from me, not waiting for my answer, beckoning to Raymond, who has just emerged from the trees. How long has he lived here? Will he just stay forever?

"See what?" I ask.

"It's right there, glowing! My God. Like it's washing ashore!" Simon cries.

"Dad, it's just the bugs again," Raymond says wearily, lighting a cigarette. "The—what's it called? The bioluminescence."

"I know this story," I say.

"It's not the damn bugs!" Simon shouts. "I know that blue when I see it!"

"Blue is only for those at the end," I whisper. "The eye of God."

"She's getting worse," Raymond says.

"Doctor says it's called sundowning," Simon responds, removing his sweater, then his shoes. "But listen, Ray, I can't deal with her now. I'm gonna row out and see what's there. Dive in if I have to!"

"For fuck's sake, now you're hallucinating, too," Raymond cries. "You have to give up on this or you'll end up just like that fool cousin of hers."

"Who's talking to whom?" Simon shouts. "Any other son worth a damn would swim out in the middle of a hurricane to save his family business rather than sit back like a goddamn louse while watching his old father do it. But you've always been a coward, Raymond—in the ocean and out of it. At the very least, you could show me a morsel of respect. After giving everything we had away to that thief loverboy of yours."

I lie down in the sand as they go on shouting. The wedding dress is gone now, and the sun rises over my near-naked body some decades in the past. Squinting my eyes, I gaze down at my torso, smooth as silk, browned by a summer nearly through. I hear my son's cry, his tiny footsteps running toward me from the beach. Just a little bit longer. I want to be alone a little bit longer here. Labor Day weekend. Two children birthed, my girlhood gone, womanhood at hand. I am wild with want. I can see them—men in multiples loving me right there on the beach, in perfumed hotel rooms, in rumbling train compartments. One after another. Gabriel, his lips tickling shapes along the fabric of my swimsuit. But then time is up, my son is upon me, sobbing, and the last phantom marauders of summer love flee the scene. My son's heart pounds against mine. He is wet with seawater. I kiss his salty hair. He is so beautiful when he cries, his eyes large as an owl's and blue, the bluest blue, black eyelashes purging tears.

"Mommy, Clarke Junior called me a fairy since I wouldn't swim out past the breakers. A fairy like Daddy, he said. Daddy's not a fairy, is he?"

"That boy doesn't know what he's talking about. Your daddy is looking for fairies in the ocean. The blue fairies."

"There's no such thing as that kind of fairy, Mother."

"Just because you can't see something doesn't mean it's not real, my dear. Am I still here when you close your eyes? Think about it. Go on. Close your eyes."

22.

Quit acting like you're dead already," Ethel yells, tying the curtains back. "Open your eyes!" The sun blazes onto the bed. I throw my hands before my face. "I'm not letting you get away with this another day," she barks on.

I touch my forehead, my temples, and find nothing attached to me. No impatient nurses press down on my head, my shoulders, my legs. I taste no rubber mouth guard. The room around me is not stifled by stainless steel, it is my own. But I shake with convulsions, little earthquakes rippling down from my brain to my toes. And then my arms go numb. "Ma-dera?" I ask her. I cannot finish the sentence, or even finish the thought.

"Oh, don't go starting on all that again. All you do is talk about the dead in vain. You outlived Doc Madera—don't you remember? He's been gone for years. Then it was just Mr. Simon feeding you those pills morning, noon, and night, like it was bread and water. I didn't need an Ivy whatchamacallit degree to know his medicine was no good. He always thought he was so smart."

I shake my head, not at what she is saying but because I cannot respond in any other way.

"Anyway, Madera's gone," she replies. "He had a terrible cancer. You got some other doctors now, but you still been callin' them all Madera."

Ethel sits down on the bed. She hums a familiar song. *Mmmm aaah mmm la deee laa.* A lullaby. Her voice has the sadness of summer's end. I want to ask her to keep singing, but my mouth will not move. Today will not last. By evening, time will have fortified its silence around me. And time is moving ever faster, because it is ending.

"I'll be darned, 'cause I might just need a head doc myself. I had a dream last night that won't let me go," Ethel says. "You wanna hear about it?" She grows frustrated, unaware I cannot answer her. "You keep shaking your head, but what's it gonna be? Yes or no?"

I say nothing, apparently, as she continues.

"Hell, no one wants to hear about anyone else's darn dreams, but I'm gonna tell you anyway, 'cause you was in it. We was out in the marsh watching the fireworks like it was the Fourth of July—that's right, your birthday. Real pretty ones, like weeping willows. And we could hear children in the distance laughing and going on with themselves. You said to me, 'Ethel, look again,' so I did, and there in the sky, made of the same pretty light as the fireworks, was my ma and also my pa. And then I saw Elijah. It's hard to describe it. Always is, them finicky dreams. And I woke up this morning just crying, 'cause at the end, right beside Elijah, I saw the baby I lost."

Ethel with child? No memory comes. But then, yes: a party, many Saturdays ago, on the brink of winter. Candlelight. Someone passes me an old-fashioned, my stomach curdles, my throat burns. I look away from the conversation and there Ethel is, at the edge of the yard, looking into the distance. She sees something I cannot. Blurred light. Her hands go to her lower belly, that protective gesture a woman instinctively makes. She is bigger there, yes. But out of propriety, I never ask after it. The blue shifts across her face. Something is in the trees. She is gazing into the end. And then: a young man, his face obscured by the passage of the years, dangles an empty glass in front of her face, then drops it. The night shatters. "Run, girl, run."

Simon, what's Clarke's boy doing over there with Ethel?

How should I know, Elle? This isn't our world. I'm sure she knows how to protect herself.

That boy is always bothering her.

"I never even told Elijah, you know that? Well, I was suspicious about it. My mama told me, when I was little, I was too witchy and badly behaved for the Lord's blessing in my womb. I thought she was right when it took so long. But then finally my belly grew and all that sickness came. Well, one night you had some sort of to-do, like you always was having in those days, for Clarke Senior's birthday. And you know how his boy liked to drink, and still do. Well, after he was good and liquored up, Clarke Junior liked to play a game in his daddy's Chrysler. We'd all heard about it up north. You know, one of those with a type he didn't like to admit to nobody, even though I was near old enough to be his mama. And so I ran and I ran from him, hiding in and out of the trees, and he didn't get me. That fool never got me, all those years he tried. But that night, when I got back north, Elijah went out with the rifle and asked me who he was gonna have to kill 'cause down my dress the blood was just coming and coming. I tried to stop it. Oh, I hated it. I prayed to every angel, but the blood kept coming and my baby came down with it.

"In my head, I told myself my mama was wrong. But in my heart I thought she was right," Ethel goes on. "Somehow I had caused it. So I never told no one about it. I reckon I told you now, because tomorrow you won't recall what I been saying. I like telling you my secrets now. It's like a confession. Back then I never even thought to blame that Clarke bastard himself—but now I do. Boy, now I do and I wish I'd let Elijah's rifle find its lawful shot."

It's not right, Simon. I'm going to say something to him. I think she's with child.

The world has never been right, my dear Elle. You can't fix it.

"Don't rush and say nothing, Elle. I don't need your pity. I don't want anyone's pity. Like Jesus said: Let the dead bury the dead. I told you because what's bothering me about the dream is, I saw something like those firework lights that night." Ethel stands and closes the curtains again, as if in a trance. "The night I lost the baby. I shoulda known they was a bad omen. Just before I went running from Clarke Junior through the woods, I saw them flickering out in your yard. I thought it was some witchery Clarke had done to the world or to me or to something I drank, but that wouldn't be the last time Clarke chased me and I learned he couldn't even pronounce a string of prayer, let alone draw some blue light 'cross the universe. I wished I shielded my eyes and sent Mr. Death back on his way, but I just kept looking, 'cause it was the prettiest thing I ever saw. Now I know the blue was Mr. Death. He was traveling through me that night. And I let him. I looked too long. You see? It's no different than diving in too deep for those gems. Just the thought makes me thirsty for something painkilling. But, like I said, it's all in the past. And I'm a rickety old woman now. Dead gotta bury their dead. Seeing those lights in the dream just made me wonder. That's all."

PART 4

Winter

23.

"Open them wider, Gabriel. I want to memorize them." I stare into Gabriel's irises, the swirling constellations there. "I have to remember exactly what your eyes look like."

His smell is the forest just after rain. I tickle the grooves of his hips, count the freckles on his arms. We are naked; our hands have no age. My hair, golden, shivers against my hips. No longer made of blood and skin and bone but of shimmering light.

"I'll just stare into the sun, Elle," Gabriel replies. "And go blind."

"But the woods are watching us," I say. "Remember?"

Gabriel sings, his voice traveling away from our bodies like the wind. And then the sun burns out. Gabriel is gone. There are no trees here. It is the sea undone. The ghosts of leaves whisper near my ear. Three owls swoop inches away from me, their wings brushing against my face. I have never seen this desert; I have never seen the end.

Ethel screams. Her voice melts this place, turns everything back to ocean. *Is your heart quiet?* Gabriel's face, a pale moon in the dark waves. There is too much water. It lashes against my calves. I can't swim. I can't swim. Where is the rope? *Gabriel!* I scream.

"Don't you let go, Elle," Ethel murmurs. "Ambulance is almost here." My room on Lyra reconfigures itself around me. She holds my hand, squeezes it. My mouth is parched like the hard desert, covered in graves. A machine crashes in the yard.

"What is?" I manage to ask. I had been dreaming of . . .

"Look, the hospital men came in a helicopter!" Ethel says. The sound of men's voices, then *boom boom boom boom*, this music of the last days of the world. The children are crying, footsteps on the stairs. *Three pills per day, not two, the world is a kingdom of blue.* The rope slipped out of my hands. It just slipped. The steel is so cold. White fluorescence. Madera's face. I'm wearing a blue gown. The nurses won't be quiet. *That woman in here yesterday should just be euthanized. There's no hope for her. Let the Lord bless her and keep her. Ladies. Ladies. No chitchat until after the anesthesia is in. Hand me the mouth guard, Ms. Johnson.* I had the rope in my grip and then . . . Gabriel, I don't know how to swim, you know that. *Count backward from ten, Mrs. Ranier.* Nine, eight, seventeen . . . *There was this light on your face. You, asleep in my lap. Light doesn't age, doesn't feel time.* The hospital lamp burns skull white, the sound of bees, soreness at the temple, my brain, my bones, no, I can't feel my body, I can't feel my body! *Mrs. Ranier, are you awake? Your therapy is finished for today. How do you feel?*

"Do you think she had a stroke?" one of the men asks Ethel, then he picks me up and lays me down on a stretcher.

"You're the doctor, ain't you?" Ethel responds.

"Holy shit," one of the men cries. My head falls to the left. An oak tree splits as if it's been struck. There is no weather but the helicopter hurling wind around the yard.

"Can't y'all watch where you land those things?" Ethel shouts. "That oak is a thousand years old."

"You coming with us in the copter?" the man shouts back at her. "If we should need someone to identify the body—"

"She ain't dead yet," Ethel spits back. Silence covers my mouth, but I know that Ethel is still holding my hand. And then we are suddenly rising together above the tree line. Around us, the blue light spreads like script through the clouds.

"What is your name?" one of the men shouts at me over the deafening sound. "What is the year? Can you count backward from ten? Do you know where you live?"

"How is she supposed to answer you if she can't hear you?" Ethel shouts back. I want to tell her that her desert is nearby. That I've seen it. "Phoenix," I say, looking at her.

"We ain't going to Phoenix," she yells at me. "In fact, I'd better pinch myself and make sure it was you not me who keeled over, 'cause I sure never seen my Lyra from such a great height."

Then it is quiet again, the quiet of dreamless sleep, that soft black country of permanent dusk. "Where?" I ask, but my throat is full of dust.

"We're stuck in this forlorn hospital on the mainland," Ethel replies.

I look at her imploringly. My voice is caught somewhere beneath my lungs. The words burn in my mouth, but I cannot say them. Something has been disconnected; they have ripped the entire architecture of English from me.

"I knew never to trust them doctors. Now they're saying you had a stroke and they won't let us leave. I tried to explain to 'em I just gave you a fright with all my storytelling about Mr. Death." I look at Ethel and notice, for the first time, how like my father's eyes hers are—far apart, as if they were meant to look not ahead but all around, to the world's ghostly periphery. And cedar-colored. I have known her since we were barely women, and only now can I pinpoint why she has always seemed so familiar. My own body, though, is unfamiliar. Wires are sunk into my veins. I try to draw my hands up, to pull the electrodes from my temples, but my arms are weak as feathers. *You ready, Dr. Madera? I'm ready. You ready, Mrs. Ranier?*

"You got nothing on your head," Ethel says. I kick my leg, but she stills me with her hand. "There, there. Simon and Ray and Zelda are on their way. Those gosh-darn blue lights—even talking about them brings Him 'round."

Gabriel lies on his side, in his room there at the edge of the property, somewhere beyond these walls. The swamp shudders. A black night spirals out above him. Even the stars shine too loud. An alligator crawls through the grass, closer. Almost upon him.

"Stop," I shout, my voice returning.

"Stop what?" Ethel asks me.

I have to warn him. I close my eyes, but instead of his room, I find myself on a train crossing the sea. The water is translucent below me, filled with cacti, pine trees, a kaleidoscope of gems. I can hear the faintest tide lapping at the rails: *cross, cross, cross.* Gabriel enters the train car. He speaks to me in another language, a language of falling rain and bells. There is a celebration on the horizon; the bells grow louder, more concentrated, marking the arrival of a new time.

I open my eyes as a picture of my mother walks toward me and sits on the bed by my side.

"Sanya," I say.

"You should rest," she says. I want to tell her how I have missed her but then all is dark, the dark of space. It is too heavy to lift myself out from this whirlpool. A man rows me out into the unknown ocean. The current grows rougher against the boat. This room of the universe looks unlike anything else, as if we are journeying into a color the human eye cannot perceive. It is so bright and so dark at once. Though we move horizontally, it feels as if we are falling backward. No desert, no breathing sky, just this cool black wind. But the ferryman shines, his skin all carnival light, and turns us in the water. "We're going back, milady," the ferryman says. "You're not finished."

Awake in a blinding room. My daughter sits beside me. There is dander in her hair, coffee stains on her teeth. She smells of the woods after a rain. If her face were a jigsaw puzzle, I could reconcile its pieces and she would appear to me as another. As Gabriel.

"I have to tell you," I say. I barely recognize my own voice. "Your father—"

But at that moment the hospital door opens again, and light bleeds in, along with Simon and his Raymond.

24.

There was a part of us that wanted another world, a twilight world, wintry and forgotten. I often imagined us living there, me and Gabriel, in that place I could not quite see—in a room the width of a tree, our bed a canoe, the walls lined with mirrors that looked out on different lands in different times. Not gravity, but music would hold us in place. The night would sing; the bells would never cease.

In the beginning, Simon left me for days to prepare his ship, the *Blue Rose*, to hunt the seas around Lyra for his treasure. Ethel left by five each afternoon, and from then until nightfall I was with Gabriel, in his arms. There in the old shed Simon had given him at the edge of the property, on the very precipice of the swamp, we made love, we slept, we made love, as the alligators growled in the grass around us. And then he carried me—running zigzag away from the beasts, as he had been advised to do—back up to the house before my husband returned. Every morning I looked over the lawn at Gabriel's quarters, afraid I'd find him torn through by alligator teeth, but that wasn't how his story ended.

Time passed. The temperature grew warmer and then colder, the alligators withdrew, and I ran home through the fall grass alone. Gabriel's body began to feel heavy, and not because he had gained weight—he had lost so much. The sadness I suffered for the rest of my life, which Madera tried to conquer, I contracted from Gabriel. His contagious melancholy, our pretty violet twilight, remained with me long after he had gone. Years after he passed, I awoke one morning to find my body had become as heavy as his. The line between us had finally vanished. Days passed into years. There were the white sheets, alternating blues in the sky, soft, pale food. Shadows on the cave wall. Simon's face, a nurse's, Ethel's. *It's one o'clock, Mrs. Ranier, time for your pill. No, Mr. Ranier says there's to be no more electroshock. It's four o'clock, time for your pill. It's January, Elle. It's April, it's July. It's 1963. It's 1987. We have entered a new millennium.* For a while, life remained in my bright dreams. Waking hurt my heart. For there were mermaids still in that other realm, a person could fly, love shook the veins, months and years and days were irrelevant, wars and pandemics did not rage, Simon's business could not fail. But in time I lost that paradise, too, and the dreams faded to murmurs. I had exhausted them; my memories had receded. It has never been pure blackness I craved, just beauty. Always beauty. Gabriel was the same.

BACK IN HIS TIME, on an evening in 1941, Gabriel stood up from the bed mid-sentence, completely naked, and walked out of the old shed into the swamp. His figure darkened as he walked on in the crepuscular light, and as the grass rose around his hips, it became difficult to distinguish him from the trees. For a few moments he stood there in the middle of that cold field, quietly beholding the early stars. But then he let out a scream that must have carried for a mile. When he had depleted his outrage, he returned to the little room as if nothing were the matter.

"What in God's name is happening to you?" I asked him. My growing fear, the obvious one, was that there was another woman somewhere, someone he had left behind, someone he now knew was not worth sacrificing to be my fake cousin. Perhaps, I thought, it could even be someone he had met on Lyra?

"How I am less than a man," Gabriel said, looking back out onto the swamp as if it stored the equation for solving all that was unfair in this life. "All I have is you. I'm just a ghost here, lying beside you. Keeping you company. Even if it makes me sick to work for Simon, at least there's purpose in it. But he has no real use for me. I suppose I'm not the type he likes around. I try and try to please him, but for some reason or another . . . he doesn't trust me. It's been the same with every boss I've ever had. A man without work though isn't a man. Back in New York, I . . . at least knew the right places to rob. I'm a thief, Elle. That's what I've always been. That's what all men are. But I'm an innocent, petty thief. Not like the rich folk. They're professional criminals. Even your Simon. How is it you think he got us both out of the draft? Whatever he did, it wasn't aboveboard, I'll tell ya. Maybe, maybe, I should go off to the war after all," he threatened. "There's some honor in dying with a weapon in your hands."

He walked back over to me, and that intangible, thick cloak of his seemed to settle upon me. "You live in this world," he went on. "You've always been better at it than me. And in this world you've got to have a roof over your head. I don't blame you for marrying Simon. You got us both a roof in the deal."

"Maybe you're right," I said, against everything I felt. "Maybe you should go. To the war or wherever. Or back to New York."

"Is that what you want, Elle?" he asked. "For once in your goddamn life, I want you to say what you want."

The dusk was complete. Soon, I knew, Simon's car would be climbing up the drive. I nodded my head, but Gabriel would not let me answer him. *This world will end one day.* He held my arms behind my body—a kind of ferociousness had returned to him—and we fell into the bed. His lips were waves upon my ears, neck, breasts. My body, within seconds, belonged completely to him.

That was the last night we ever made love. All I would keep from it is the pang of his hand, after pausing on my back or my belly, removing itself forever. The way he spoke to me throughout, imperceptibly, beneath his breath, words I'll never hear again, so opposite to the force of his body, which was torrential, like his life was giving way.

And he had given me Zelda.

I had never slept in his arms. That night, by accident, I found myself in them still come dawn. Gabriel was watching me, willing me to wake. I opened my eyes and saw a firefly light just above his forehead, then disappear. It was the last of its kind.

"I didn't think we had fireflies down here," I said.

"I told you already, Elle, those ain't lightning bugs," Gabriel replied. "They're fairies."

"Did you sleep at all, Professor?" I asked him.

"With my eyes open," he said. "So no dream could steal this memory."

But the moment was ending. Life beyond us was returning. The curtains turned gray in the rising light, fluttering there. It became a memory as soon as I took notice of it at all—the perfume that came with the dawn wind, our own scent, the amalgam of our bodies. "Gabriel, I have to go," I said.

"Oh, let the whole world burn," he replied. "Let him murder us." Still, he lifted me off the mattress and started running me home in his mad dash through the morning. The birds were already up chirping, gossiping over our affair. My heart was pounding with fear. Simon would see us; we would be found out. Gabriel's lips were moving, his depression temporarily evaporated, but I was not listening. I leapt out of his arms and up the long stairway, into the house.

On the dining table waiting for me was a note sent by messenger the night before: *Promising sight due east. Staying on the ship tonight. See you around lunchtime. Love, S.*

Weeks passed. I did not need a doctor to tell me what was causing my spells of nausea, the lack of blood in the middle of the month.

Quicksand had crawled inside our love. Soon I would be swollen. And Simon and I had still not consummated our marriage. The road had split ahead of me. I could choose to be free, live the vagabond life with Gabriel, digging in rubbish for our next meal. Perhaps run off to Los Angeles, as he'd always wanted, and find fame in Hollywood as George and Isabelle. But there would be no true revolution. I was a married woman and with child. I was only Elle Cumberland, a simple person with no extraordinary talent beyond a temporarily pretty face. The real threat was being forced to make a decision at all. To leave was a choice. To stay was to just stay. Most people stay in the world that has been chosen for them. Without Gabriel, I was no different from most people. The days I made love to him, my face changed in the mirror, had a supernatural glow. But that was Gabriel's residue—his courage, his madness. He was the one who lived on the precipice. I have always lingered behind him. I have always remained human.

Simon drank profusely in our first year together, perhaps to avoid having to lie with me. Finally, I used his intoxication to my advantage. In those early weeks, before I was showing, Simon returned home, stumbling drunk. I poured him another Scotch and another, until he collapsed atop our blankets, glass in hand, his cigar still smoking. I pried off his underwear, then dropped my own atop his. I straddled my legs over his pale, elegant body and pressed his penis into me, all soft, barely alive. After a few moments, he shivered slightly. So different from Gabriel, even in this—so much more restrained, more refined. It had happened at last. It would happen like that a few more times in our life together.

In the morning, Simon's face was pale when we awoke naked beside each other. "Darling," he said. "Was everything all right?"

"It was," I said.

"But are you hurt?" Simon asked.

"You could never hurt me," I said.

Later that week, Gabriel emerged in the garden like a spook, wan and thin, as I attended to the roses. "You haven't come to me in days and days," he whispered harshly. "You've been avoiding me."

I once believed that a baby comes into this world the instant a man and woman make love. But it isn't true. A baby is conceived hours later, once the act itself is already a memory. Life is made in the aftermath of love, in its departure. Once it is already of the past.

"I can't come to you every day, Gabriel," I replied, like he was only a hired hand. "You forget sometimes that I am a married woman."

25.

On Zelda's seven-and-three-quarters birthday, at the start of the prosperous fifties, she wandered out of her room and into one of our endless dinner parties—a party stilted by that perfect pitch of polite and animated chatter on the economy and the president and how much we longed for the last president, though we had despised that one in his time, too, a party I had spent three days preparing for, the salad, the cheeses, the custard, the candles, the wine, the flowers—to announce the advent of her new age, how close she was to eight, displaying that saddest quirk of youth, a longing to grow up. We applauded dear Zelda and then quickly banished her back to the island of childhood so we could return to clinking our glasses and worrying over our savings bonds. By the end of the night, Simon was drunk enough to pat one of our guests, a lawyer we never saw again, on the thigh one too many times, upon which Mayor Clarke and his wife bade us a polite and knowing adieu, while Simon drew the beloved lawyer out to have a look at the garden and back in to sit for a tune on the piano, saying over and over how much the handsome lawyer resembled an actor whose name he couldn't remember, until the lawyer and his wife politely excused themselves, too. Simon said farewell to our guests, then poured himself another glass of Scotch, still aglow with the perfume of flirtation. "Well, they were nice, after all, weren't they? And he was just so refined, so intelligent. I must say I don't understand what he could see in her."

I couldn't bear his maniacal chatter and slipped away from him onto the porch for a cigarette, when I heard my lonely girl talking to herself, crouching between the trees in the garden, telling her secrets to the holes in the bark. Zelda had invented a magical language, one her mother was only sometimes allowed to hear. I remained undetected as I approached, to hear her whisper into the oak: *Abracadabra sotto voi shira ba boom.* Somehow her seven-and-three-quarters-year-old brain had conjured a language that sounded, at least, like a mélange of Latin and Italian and nonsense.

By the time I reached her pale, slight body, brightened by the full moon, Zelda had turned her attention away from the oak and was holding her arms up toward the sky, casting spells to an ocean fairy she favored, though sometimes the fairy was a mermaid instead. The fairy often had messages for Zelda, which Zelda was not allowed to relay, lest she arouse the anger of the ocean assembly.

The moon was spectacular that night, another world appearing in the atmosphere of our own. It seemed to stir the entire island—the birds burned with chatter, the dogs howled their sad, old song—but most of all my little angel would not hear of going to bed. "Mother, it's time for me to go to the ball," Zelda whined.

"And which ball is that, my darling?" I asked. She was very serious about her parties. "It's past midnight. You are supposed to be sleeping."

"The ball at the center of the ocean, where all the fairies are going tonight," Zelda replied.

"Is that right?" Simon chuckled. He had found us in the garden while taking a saunter with his *last* drink of the evening.

"Yes." Zelda grew serious. "No adults are allowed at the ball because they aren't allowed to meet fairies. I'm sorry." She looked at us sympathetically.

"Isn't it time for you to be in bed, sweetheart?" Simon asked.

"How can I go to sleep if I'm expected at the ball? Balls don't happen in the daytime!" Zelda grew very flustered, but Simon was no longer laughing. Zelda's fantasies often troubled him, as if he sensed in them some obscure ill omen. He had taken to urging her to become more "efficient" and "productive," even though she was only seven and three-quarters.

"Don't you want to be productive tomorrow?" Simon asked.

"I'm not tired," she whimpered. Zelda pulled my arm. "*Mother* . . ." she said, extending the word so that it seemed to capture more than just our biological relation, embracing some kind of obligation to indulge her. "I have to show you something."

Simon shook his head and left us to ourselves. Zelda took off in the opposite direction, skipping through the woods ahead of me. “Slow down, dear!” I screamed. “Stay in the garden!”

But she ran on. As the moonlight slivered down through the oak, I felt my way by hand, the moss slipping through my fingers, whereas Zelda knew by heart the path to the sea. The woods' small movements whispered like ghosts. There were phantoms, not fairies, in every direction.

At last, standing on the white dunes, I saw Zelda's small body, the size of a fairy herself, beside the black ocean. I screamed her name, but the wind carried my voice in the other direction. I feared she would walk into the sea and I would have to go after her, unable to swim, and, in drowning, find her father.

“You have to come all the way down to the water,” Zelda shouted, already toeing the surf. “For me to show you, you have to come here.”

“Zelda, this game is over. Do not go any farther,” I screamed, running toward her. The sand was damp and cool.

“My fairy friend wants me to tell you that you can go into the ocean without being afraid.”

“I am not afraid of the ocean, you silly girl,” I said. “But you better be afraid of me. You are in a whole lot of trouble.”

“She says just lie down in it, in the shallow water, and let the water go over you. Don't try to swim,” Zelda said, ignoring my admonitions.

“I'm not going into the water, Zelda,” I said. “And neither are you.”

"But that's the only way to get to the ball, Mother. We just have to sit in the shallow part."

Zelda was talking to me like I was one of her dolls. And then she ran out into the waves. My heart leapt. "Come back this instant, Zelda!" But she was walking farther, the ocean up to her calves. She had the blind determination of her father.

"We just have to sit right here," she screamed. "Please don't make me miss it."

Where we were, the sea was flat and soft. The moon cast a reflection like a road out to the Rapture, a pathway knowable for only that one night. My old longing to take it returned—to rediscover that more perfect place, the dreaming ocean.

"Seri voce baboomm kria auria auriqui!" Zelda squealed. "Now lie down in the water so we can go to the ball!"

Her spell had been cast. We lay holding hands as the smallest of waves crested over our shoulders. The salt was all stars, the water silk on my skin. Then, suddenly, it was past us—it was over. We were breathing. That was Zelda's grand affair.

"Get up, Mommy. Did you dance with any of the fairies?" she asked sincerely.

"Yes, they danced like this!" I said, waving my arms like a pair of wings.

"You're so silly. The fairies don't have wings. They fly by using their umbrellas," Zelda corrected me. "Now that you've met the fairies, you get to know the most important secret of all," she went on. "But I have to whisper it in your ear." I leaned down into the sweet cup of her small hands.

"The fairies told me that my real father is a fairy king who lives in the middle of the ocean. You were once almost a fairy, too, but you decided to stay human. One day you'll be a mermaid fairy, though, and you'll reunite with the fairy king."

"And how do you get to be the fairy king or queen?" I asked, indulging her.

"It's simple, really. You have to drown in the ocean."

26.

We are back on Lyra, Simon and I, staring at the Atlantic. I look down to find myself seated in a wheelchair. "Happy to be home?" he asks me.

Lacking the will to complain, I nod my head. The surf surges toward us, reaching for our feet. The ocean wears a different face today. This steely winter ocean is my favorite. The summer sea is gaudy, a showgirl, but in this last season, it belongs only to me.

"A week in the hospital isn't a vacation," Simon says. "At least the chair's just temporary."

"Am I cured?" I ask him, relieved that at the least I'll walk again.

"Well, you can speak," he says. He has not brought his papers with him today. I have known him long enough to know that this signals there's something we are meant to discuss here.

"What's on your mind?" I ask. Overhead the clouds are inky, swollen. Soon they will defeat our little outing with rain.

"I was thinking of when I almost drowned as a kid," he says. "And also, of how I wished I'd gone swimming more here."

"That was with your brother. . . . He held you down, didn't he?"

"Good memory," he says sarcastically. "You know Joe's sick?" He is testing me. "It isn't kind to speak badly of the ill. Deb says he'll go any day now. But I hate him much more than I love him, at this point." Simon takes my hand in his, draws an infinity symbol with his finger on my wrist. "Thank God I've had you. Better than a brother or a sister. I should have listened to you when you told me to stick to my guns about the business."

"What would have happened if you'd have stuck to your guns?" I ask.

"We'd never have manufactured the Caeruleum. I'd have died looking for those jewels. I suppose we'd still have lost all our money. The end would have come sooner but been the same," he says. "The only difference is, maybe you'd never have . . ." The rest of Simon's thought falls into the wind. "Do you think your mother is alive, Elle?"

I shake my head and meditate on the tug of the ocean. *She's everywhere now.* Lurking beneath even the calmest surface is the void itself—that plummet through stars, ocean fairies. "My mother has been dead almost as long as I've been on this planet."

"You thought so this morning," he goes on. "The entire time in the hospital, you called Zelda by her name. Called her Sanya. And Raymond—you won't even address him directly." I have so rarely seen Simon cry, but here come his tears. "And I can't stop thinking it's all my fault. I mean, you might have gotten sick without the Caeruleum. . . . All our life together, I wanted to just find the answer. I just wanted you to wake up one day without that weight on your chest. That gray aura haunting your eyes. Happy. The way you were when we were kids. I thought that's what you wanted, too, that that was why you put up with the ECT and then the Caeruleum. I thought you wanted to be saved. I mean, doesn't everyone want to feel better?"

"I don't recall ever arguing about it," I say.

"Just yesterday at the hospital, you threw a fit about how I'd ruined your entire life, Elle. With the help of Madera, of course. Your favorite villain."

"What's yesterday when you are old?" I reply. It is suddenly very funny to me. Yesterday's gone. Gone as what washes up in the tide and is carried back to sea. I try to suppress my laughter, but it feels too good. Soon it will all be washed away, the memory of our ever having been here. Good riddance. Let the ocean devour it.

"I've spent my whole life thinking about tomorrow," Simon says. "What's going to happen tomorrow? And now there's nothing to see there. It's all in yesterday." He stands up, Scotch in hand, and starts to do a little jig in the sand. He has a small limp now, in his left leg. I can smell, on his skin, the scent of my father's final years. How must I look to him?

"Also, I never found them," Simon says, kneeling down and pulling a fragment of seashell from the sand. "I wanted to place around your neck the most magnificent rock any woman had ever seen. Every morning I woke up with the notion. That that very day I would dig out those gems—Elle, you are still the most beautiful woman I've ever seen. From the first time I saw you, at the old shop in New York . . ." Simon drowns the rest of the memory in his drink. "Perhaps that was the right answer all along. Just to find the jewels for you. Nothing else."

"My former glory isn't why you brought me down here today, is it, Simon?" I ask.

"Elle, you go in and out. But you're really here today, aren't you?" he asks, and I return his gaze as reassuringly as an ailing woman can. "There's a lot that's been happening—that I've lost control of, you might say. I've missed confiding in you about it. Well, the north end of the island's abandoned. It's a ghost town up there. Clarke Junior's developers bought everyone out of their homes. Ethel's been living with us—kindest woman there ever was—but I've got to let her go. We've got to live simpler now." He tilts the glass to his lips, barely noticing it is dry.

"And, oh God, Elle, I've had to sell the house. That's what I couldn't bear to tell you. We had to pay back the creditors after the Caeruleum recall. That Clarke boy made millions on some mumbo-jumbo dot-com I don't understand. He even got Ray involved with some folks out west, told him to invest in some robot nonsense that failed miserably. And once Clarke Junior knew we were completely done for, he made the offer for the house in cash. How could I refuse him, Elle? He's interested in the Caeruleum, too. Says he'll bring me back on as an adviser. Something about portable phones

I don't understand. The fool thinks the future is all in machines."

Simon has been avoiding my gaze, but now he looks me in the eye. "Elle, we have until the end of the month in the house. I'm so sorry."

"We used to come out here when you had good news to tell me," I say, trying to make Simon laugh. "Will the horses be allowed to remain, at least?"

One fine day, the world will be left to the horses, when the planet decides at last there have been too many of us. I imagine it is all the horses have ever wanted, to run free on the ever-diminishing land, and all we have ever done is beat them down and entrap them. But nature will have its solution for them, too, and when the ocean sweeps over all this, the horses, native to the steppes of another land, will find their last graves in the Atlantic. Perhaps the ocean might show them some grace, transform them into seagoing unicorns, and they will go on, galloping gorgeously beneath the waves. In a few centuries, if we survive at all, it will be as mermaids, ocean fairies. And at last, after it's too late for us to realize we were never alone, some extraterrestrial ship will pass over this cul-de-sac of our galaxy, peer over the heaving blue, and recognize it as the ultimate living thing, ignoring that beneath it lies the wreckage of less advanced intelligences: humans, horses, Lyra. And then they will sail on.

"I hope they'll leave them be," I reply on Simon's behalf.

"I've been having these recurring dreams," Simon says. "You're in the sky above me. And I'm below you in this frozen landscape. You're flying, but it looks like you're swimming, swimming through the clouds, and there is nothing else but you." He looks at me and takes my withered hands in his. "Let's have one last party here, Elle. Fireworks and all. I know you love a good party. What do you say?"

27.

The branches shiver and shed blue light, as trees elsewhere shed snow. This new weather slithers up through Ethel's hands as she braids my hair. I look in the mirror and see where the light enters and leaves my skull, enters and leaves my lungs, falling through the rest of me as it behaves in the trees. "Can you see it?" I ask Ethel.

"I can barely see an inch ahead of me," she replies. Her hair has turned so white. There is no black left in it. So short a time ago, we were just girls. "But you know I always say seeing is like Mary Magdalene going to the tomb of Christ and finding out it's empty. The ears are more reliable."

I ask Ethel when she will leave Lyra.

"Well, I had planned on dying here like my mama and daddy," she replies. "But since nobody asked my opinion about selling the island off to Mayor Clarke's damnable offspring, and I don't plan on having him for my eternal company, I was thinking 'bout using my savings to go west. Like I told you, to Phoenix, Arizona. Cheap land. Never rains. Sun is always shining. I want to get far away while I can. I can't just live on the shores of Georgia forever, knowing they took everything. That's how Moses died, an inch from glory."

"Our house didn't burn like the others," I say. "I always waited for it to."

"You can't ever tell what God has in store, for Lyra or any of us," Ethel replies. "Now stop fidgeting and let me braid your three strings of hair."

For a moment, in her hands, I fall into the ocean and find my mother and father. Just past shore, the water is already deep. I stretch my toes down to the bottom, but there is nothing, no floor. Thousands of graves float in the water. The sea changes color from red to purple to blue to red, as if it suffers its own sunset. There is an event we are all swimming toward. My father cups my hand in his. "I feel so very sad," he says.

"You'd better get out of this old night slip!" Ethel sighs, returning me here. "It's almost time for the party!"

THEY ARRIVE IN THE HUNDREDS. I go out among them, candlelight shines in their glasses, a dull remembrance of a name, what happened between us, who we have been to one another, which one of us always drank too much. There is a band, saxophone, trumpet, trombone, dancing, shattered glasses, curses, laughter. I navigate the circus in a wheelchair. For a moment, in the dim light, I am the only one among them who has grown old. Time has touched only me and my demolished garden. They are gathered around all the cocktail tables. Cheeks red with cheer. I have done it. I have made them all happy. I have become a Ranier.

My girl approaches, very drunk, tripping down the steps. Her glittering dress drags in the wet mud. "Mommy, you look so clear tonight," she says through hiccups. "It all looks like it used to . . . except the people. I wish there were more people like there used to be here. There was always so many, many people."

Oh, will you smell that cake? It's Elle's famous chocolate cake! She says she does it herself. How can a woman bake chocolate like that and stay so slim?

My mother's face. The years spin backward to 1926. A bar of chocolate on the bedside stand. *Let her memory of me be sweet, my David.* Every afternoon I take another nibble at it, as if it were a wonderful story that I never want to end. Then all that is left is the wrapper. I ask my father when my mother is coming back. *Oh, honey, she's not,* he says. *She's not coming back. She's an angel. She's everywhere now. Like the ocean.*

Even earlier: My hands are in theirs. My mother and father, Sanya and David. A woman walks hastily ahead of us with an umbrella for shade, a red picnic basket in her hands. The sun is resplendent. I fall beneath her canopy. Embroidered there is a land of enchantment—a faraway land, where once upon a time ancient emerald woods met crystal dunes and the blue sea. My mother squeezes my hand, says something to me in Russian. Then looks at my father. This is my very first memory of the world. I close my eyes and fall through the cobblestone road back to Lyra.

"Make a wish!" someone shouts. In my hands, a feast of chocolate again. Laughter and wind come for the candles. They sputter, then return. A man kneels before me. His hands are rough, but they handle me so gently. He sets my braids aside, then places a necklace over my head. I look down upon it, its blue burning heart. My sight blurs. *Gabriel. But is it you?*

The voice of a woman occludes him. *Elle, did you do the flowers tonight? Why, you should run the florist's shop yourself! Not that you need to, with Simon out on that ship every day hunting treasure.*

The smell of lilies returns. Their perfume of moonlight. Everywhere I look, daffodils, roses, tulips. It's spring, and I walk between my mother and father, and the strange woman's umbrella has just made a left turn into oblivion. The sun burns my face. And I begin to weep. It is gone, my enchanted land. My mother squeals with delight, paying me no attention. My father has stolen a blue rose for her.

I hear my girl talking with a group nearby. Something about a Gordon, about his time away . . .

"Second chances are important," a man responds. His hand clings to my shoulder.

"Well, Ray, this is not a second chance. This is a third strike. More like a fourth or fifth, really," says a familiar voice behind me.

"He's ill, Simon," my girl says. "No different than what Mom's sick with."

"If he's so ill, Zelda, why then does he refuse treatment?" the older man replies.

"Oh, like you're the big expert!" she cries. "Perhaps I should dose him up with Caeruleum after a few rounds of ECT and see what happens."

"Remember Mom's fiftieth?" the blue-eyed young man interjects. "There were so many people here that night. Do you think anyone else is coming? It's like they've all forgotten—"

"We had parties for every occasion!" my girl cries back. "Not just her fiftieth. She was always overdoing it. Fireworks. Champagne. God, the money you two spent. To think, the entire island and all their third cousins once removed were feasting on our backs."

"Those were the golden days. Just look at what the Clarkes have done to this garden," the older man says from behind me. "It's like a war zone. I don't understand why they have to tear everything up. Why they've got to destroy everything we made."

"Don't get all maudlin," my girl says. "You wallow in the past worse than her sometimes."

"The past is all that's left to the old, dear Zelda," the gentleman replies. "One day you'll understand and you won't have us around to console you."

I look down at my neckline. The jewel from the handsome stranger is gone. I clutch at my chest.

"What's she doing?" my girl asks.

"Everything's missing," I say.

"I know, sweetheart," the older man says to me, his face coming into view. "I know. But we'll get it back." Then he turns to the rest of the group, lowers his voice to a hush. "I'll tell you, since he stopped drinking, Clarke Junior's turned into some kind of robot. I don't think he's still got real blood knocking around underneath that skin. He was talking to me yesterday about using the Caeruleum deposits for some kind of telephone device. Straightfaced, says these things could have about a jillion times the memory of the human brain. No more worrying about our, and I quote, 'entropic carcasses.' Like he doesn't know my own wife, the woman who was like a godmother to him—"

"Doesn't he know the Caeruleum causes—you know, *rapid onset*?" my girl asks. "His big plan sounds pretty counterintuitive."

"They never proved causation," the younger man responds quickly. "Besides, Clarke's in technology, not pharmaceuticals. You can't get dementia from holding a phone to your face."

"Well, he was quite gabby with me today," my girl says, changing the subject. "Told me I'm welcome to visit anytime, like the goddamn place has always been his. Can't believe the Clarkes couldn't be bothered to show up tonight, of all nights. . . ."

"They could have come just for her," the older gentleman says, eyeing the younger man. "She used to get so nervous at the beginning, before people really started coming. And now no one will ever come again."

"What do you believe, Ma?" the young man says, turning his attention toward me. "Do you still believe there's some magic out there in the ocean, like you used to?"

I want this dream to end, I wish to reply as the blue light disperses across the garden in falling stars or fireworks. Their voices grow muffled beneath it. And another is just beside me. He surrounds me like music. *See, Elle. It didn't take so long to get here. Let's just live on this beach at the end of the world.*

Gabriel, but what about all these strange carnival people?

Oh, darling, but you're in love with a regular tramp. Isn't that what you love about me? I'm free.

"Mom, raise your glass for the toast!" my girl screams.

The young man stands beside her, a guitar in his hands. His voice is so mild, like the breeze in April. "Let's sing together, okay, Ma?" he asks me and begins to strum a few familiar chords. "We'll do your favorite song."

The guests twirl around me as if on a carousel; my girl stumbles, her champagne spilling. The music touches all the chandeliers in the universe. And the lyrics pour out of me: "I'll be coming home—wait for me . . ."

"Mommy!" It's my Zelda. I turn and look for her like I might find her five years old again, clutching her nightgown, looking for her four-leaf clover.

"Yes, angel?" I say.

"Have you really come back?" she asks.

I gaze out upon Lyra, which still astounds me, even after all this time. The light fairies through the air, recasting the island in blue, violet, blue. Down the tumbling lawn, past the abandoned wooden tables, is the tiered pagoda where I was married. And just beyond the shuttered pool lie the ruins of the former mansion, that circle of stones—a vision of the past and future at once. Then my favorite part of all begins: the congregation of emerald oak and the ocean beyond. One can stand beneath the low shade of the woods, just before those dunes of fallen stars, and never know the Atlantic is there at all. But it has been there, just beyond my garden, all these long years, waiting for me.

PART 5

28.

I sit beside the sun-drenched window, desperate as any house cat that was never, not once, let out of doors. Our curtains have fled. Our nightstands, our bureaus, our paintings, our china, our dining table, our lampshades, our trinkets, our dresses, our suits, our stashes of jasmine tea, have all deserted us. The house shivers with loneliness. Piles of boxes line the hallways. The only smells that remain are cardboard and must. Doors slam. All the wind has been let in. The house has forsaken gravity. It will just float away. *Simon got a fine price*, someone whispers. It feels like the changing of seasons, but from when to when, I no longer know. It is warm enough.

A crow perches on the windowsill, some warning of the darker future. I close my eyes and return instead to the old cemetery in New York. At last it feels like spring, but the grass is cold from the melting of the frost. Still, there shines the sun, warm on our stupidly bare skin. Our legs are intertwined. The red in his beard gleams in that sudden April. My hands spread over his back and I draw him closer to me. I have forgotten he has only just recently made me angry. But for what?

"Lyra," Gabriel says. "Like the constellation. With Cygnus it forms the Summer Triangle."

"The train leaves at seven in the morning," I say, interrupting his lecture.

He kisses my mouth shut. "The train isn't leaving."

Gabriel is so close to me, I notice a small pimple forming on his inner eyelid. In the morning it will hurt him, I know. Everything will.

"I can't bear to ever see you sad on account of me," I say.

"Well, chérie, I'll try not to die from it," Gabriel replies. "Besides, we won't be staying there long, right?"

"Oh, just a couple of centuries," I say jokingly.

"You promised me, Elle Bell."

AND THEN IT WAS MORNING. I stood between the two of them, wary of being too close to Gabriel. Simon shook his hand vigorously. "The famous cousin!"

"I'm so grateful for the opportunity." Gabriel's voice changed. Suddenly I was being held in Simon's arms. "I'd been meaning to get back down to a warmer climate."

"Oh, I'm sure you will be very happy on the island." Simon's voice was too sweet and his arms were so thin. I felt like a giant in his embrace. "Funny, you two don't look a lick alike. Of course, that might be because Elle is so very beautiful," Simon said. "No offense to you, Gabe. Can I call you Gabe?"

Gabriel hated the nickname. "I take after my father, she her mother," Gabriel said quickly. "And, sir, you can call me anything you like."

"Elle, I couldn't get a ticket for Gabe in first class," Simon said to me. What did my face do then? I'll never see it. But Gabriel rescued me from it.

"Oh, it's quite all right, sir," Gabriel said. "I'll see you two lovebirds on the other side of the rainbow."

29.

And what was that day like for Gabriel—the last day he lived? I hunted for him but could not find him until evening fell. Our child was swelling inside of me. One moment my blood rioted with anger, the next I collapsed in tears. I hated him that day; I needed him. I paced back and forth between the house and his shed, barefoot and mad, not minding for alligators, pushing his door open to find only his empty bed. This might have struck a wiser woman as foreshadowing, but I had lost my wisdom. I was a mere mammal, searching the earth for my mate.

He had left first thing in the morning, or even in the middle of the night, to where I'll never know. Perhaps Simon had finally assigned him a task that called him off the property. More likely he spent the day pacing, just as I was, up and down the wilds of the island, escaping the burden of encountering another human face.

I have tried for so long to remember the sound of his voice that evening when I finally found him, there on the unlighted beach. He nodded to the boat, then pulled his blue shirt off and left it on the shore, offering a cursory explanation that the shirt was done for, had a hole. I thought once again that he had some mad trick up his sleeve, that he might blow us up with fireworks or row me out until forever, to Bermuda and then the Canary Islands, from there to the coast of Africa, where the desert meets ocean.

"I want to talk to you, Elle," he said. His voice cracked. "Out there. I want to show you something."

"Can't we talk on the beach, Gabriel?" I insisted. "I've been searching for you all day."

"It feels better to be out on the water," he said. "Like we could go somewhere." I have said those words to myself every day since, walking through the breathing woods, during silent dinners with Simon, every single time I look at the Atlantic. *Like we could go somewhere.* "Just for a little bit. Just to be you and me. Isabelle and George."

"What do you want to show me, Gabriel?"

"It's a surprise, Elle," Gabriel whispered. "One you have to keep a secret."

"Fine," I said. And he helped me into the boat, like a princess to her carriage, and rowed me out into the darkness. What remains after we left shore is the residue of a dream. The ocean was hushed and black. I lay in his arms, against his bare chest, and felt that warmth, that irreplaceable hunger in my blood to be near him, as close as possible, intertwined with him, to dissolve into him—wasn't that animal feeling the very zenith of human emotion? I have never since felt so alive.

We were quickly far from shore. The tide had pushed us out without our noticing it. The wind was cold off the ocean, raising the hairs on my arms. Gabriel was rubbing my legs, and then his hands went there, to my belly, which had risen, noticeably, and he almost knew, and he began to hum to her. I looked up. Suddenly the night had become brilliant with stars. In our little rowboat in the middle of the black Atlantic, billions of years of light had arrived just for us. Gabriel was whispering in my ear, speaking dimly of things I try to remember now—those words, all of these years—but cannot. It has been like having a conversation with a figure in a dream. And then . . .

"Do you see that blue light all through the trees on the coast of Lyra?" Gabriel asked. "It's everywhere, actually."

I looked up to where he had pointed, my head nestled in the crook of his neck, his smell all burned wood, Gabriel himself mixing with the salt and the wind off the sea. "You mean the stars?" I asked. "I just see little stars."

Gabriel lifted himself up and I slipped off his chest. "Seriously. Look back over at Lyra. That's where you can see it best. See how all the oaks are twinkling blue?"

I looked to shore. "What have you had to drink tonight?" I said, laughing, but his breath was clean, sweet. Lyra's silhouette was dark and ever more distant.

"Remember when we first met, Elle?" he asked, then went on. "On the A train. You were sitting beside me, nose turned up, and my first impression of you was that you were a prude. Then, out of nowhere, you collapsed in my lap. I thought you'd fainted but you—you'd just fallen asleep there like you knew me all your life. Like a total madwoman."

"How could I ever forget when all you do is tease me about it?" I replied.

"I wouldn't dare wake you. I just watched you, mesmerized, as dreams formed beneath your eyelids. Your face kept moving through all these expressions: sadness, anger, bliss, sadness. Some seconds you looked like you might start crying, and others like you were laughing. But I fell for you when I saw the way you looked sad. Even asleep, it was already like I'd known you all my life. That's how familiar you were to me. I missed my stop without noticing. Then the train rose up and we were in Brooklyn. There was this light on your face. . . . I couldn't describe it then but now I see it everywhere I look. You see, light is the only thing that doesn't age. It's the only thing that doesn't feel time." Gabriel kissed me. Our lips were both chapped from the wind. It was the driest kiss we ever shared, and our last.

"Now you've made our meeting sound like one of your fairy stories," I said.

"Isn't that what you love about me?" Gabriel replied. "The world out there is a sort of prison, but in my stories fairies fly. And we are free."

"Your stories are ridiculous," I said.

"Let me tell you another, then. A truly fantastic one," Gabriel said. "You know those gems Simon's looking for—well, they're far more brilliant than he's let on. They sit down there under the water, reflecting a map of all of the stars above. And when you have one in your hands, your soul becomes visible. What you're really made of. You see, if I had one on a ring right now, and I put it on your finger, I could—"

"And what are our souls made of, Professor Bell?" I asked, interrupting his mad soliloquy.

"Blue luminescence," he replied very seriously.

"Blue luminescence," I repeated, as if I knew they were words I must always remember. "Okay, I know how it begins. But how does it end, your story?"

"Like it always does," Gabriel replied. "The prince and the princess—or, in this case, you and I—we live happily ever after. You see, Elle Bell, out here, well, nobody owns the ocean. And besides, I've beaten Simon to it. It just so happens I've already found Simon's treasure. By the end of the night you'll be dressed in gems—like I promised you long ago. That's why I brought you here. The jewels are all around us. Right below us. All we gotta do is dive in and get them. Go ahead and look down—can't you see 'em?"

30.

Mrs. Ranier," Elijah said, his voice paled by the sad strum of the sea. "What're you doing out here all alone?" I opened my eyes and realized for the first time that the night had broken for a violet morning. On land the birds were chirping, bells were chiming. Hours must have passed since Gabriel dove beneath the water.

Elijah extended the oar from his boat into mine, to prevent me from drifting away. "Mrs. Ranier, you all right?"

My dress was still wet, frozen against my legs. Elijah leapt into the boat and wrapped me in his coat. I felt I should not speak, as speaking might wake me up. The awful dream would belong to the day; it would be real.

"Mrs. Ranier, come on now, say something."

"My cousin Gabe—he went looking for something." I shivered through the words.

"In the ocean? In the middle of the night?" Elijah asked. I nodded my head. "That boy don't listen."

"Blue and shining, he said. Like a kingdom down there," I said.

"He said he hadn't been drinking." The sun was suddenly high above us.

Elijah jumped out of the boat and swam around it, dipping down under the surface and up again.

"We'll do a search," Elijah said once he returned to the boat, lifting himself into it with one motion. "We might still find the body."

"The body?" I screamed. Gabriel could not be dead. Death was not the end of his story.

"I'm sorry, ma'am," he replied. "Mr. Gabe went looking too deep."

Then Elijah was gone. Where am I now? I press Gabriel's blue shirt to my face. It was almost lost to the surf. It smells of his sweat. Tick tock, the grandfather clock. Knock knock, Elijah's knock. It's nighttime again. *No body*. A sensation of being beaten all over by wings. *Elle, they're only twenty feet down, at most. Can't you see 'em? Gabriel Gabriel Gabriel, no. Come with me, Elle. Just hold my hand. We'll go just halfway to get a better look. I won't let you drown. No, Gabriel. I'll tie us together with this rope and tie the rope to the boat. I just felt something against my thigh, Gabriel. This is insane, Gabriel. There's nothing here that can hurt us, Elle. The sharks are all sleeping. I've got you. No, you go ahead, Gabriel. Go without me. I'll hold the rope. Why don't you believe in me, Elle? Why do you always give up on me? I can't see anything, Gabriel. I promise you they're right there, Elle. You go. Okay, Isabelle, just don't let go of me*. My belly full,

full of light. I keep hold of the boat, the rope. I'm with child, I want to say, never say. He kicks up small waves as he dives down deeper, waves I can feel beneath my feet. The tug of him in my hands. His gravity. The silent ocean. Just echo, just the eternity of water. Fear turns my belly. My belly full, full of bats. The water howls. I jump back into the little wooden boat, hull beneath me, a gust of wind overhead. And the rope, the rope slips out of my shaking hands.

It slithers down. So quickly. The black sea takes it. Like it never was. And now the house is empty. What has happened? Where has everything gone?

"Where am I?" I scream.

Someone's face comes into view, like a shadow against the bright sun. "Home," she says. "Lyra."

"Has Elijah found Gabriel yet?" I ask her.

"Elijah was my husband," she says. "He's not been with us for some time." She sits on the windowsill beside me. Her hands wander through my hair. "I'm Ethel, remember?"

"It was a mistake," I whimper. "I wasn't supposed to let the rope go. He was supposed to come right back up."

"What rope, honey?" After a moment, she stands up again. "Soon you'll be on your way out of here and to Savannah. A real town, just like New York. Mr. Simon got you a pretty house over there. And all this, all them ropes, will just be past."

Ethel is on her way somewhere else. Desert, the ancient soul of the ocean. A hush falls over it at dusk. "Phoenix," I say aloud.

"Yes, I'm heading to Phoenix soon enough," she says. "Can't be like Lot's wife all our lives. We've just got to not look back. I've got to get released of all this memory. They say that's what the West is good for."

And soon enough, I will hear her footsteps shuffle down the hall. I know by heart that sound. She has said good evening to me at this blue hour, as the day slips into night, for sixty years—but never like this, never for the last time. "I remember back when Elijah told me Gabriel went and died for that blue shiny," she says. "And I said to Elijah, 'Well, he was a doggone fool after all, wasn't he? Crazier than we thought.' And as I'm sayin' all this, this look was goin' through Elijah's eyes. Real mournful-like. Like he was saying back: 'I'm a doggone fool, too, Ethel. I ain't no wiser than that boy.'"

Ethel retreats from me, then pauses at the door. "But you know, Ms. Elle, up north what we always said is that that place is more beautiful than the most beautiful dreams, so beautiful it sends all this world to cinders. Lord, I pray Elijah got to see what Gabriel did when he chose to leave me all alone here. I pray every day he did.

"I'm gonna be making my way now," Ethel continues. "On toward the sunset. But before I do, I've got to light that flaming sword behind me. My mama used to say: 'Sometimes it's left to us to do God's work here on Earth. Keep His paradise safe from those who would'—well, maybe by now you understand our Lyra.

"Farewell for now, Elle Bell. I'll be seeing you in the kingdom come."

31.

The evening before Lyra burns, out of a land in this world to a land in the next, a soul is returned to Earth after wandering the lonely towns of other galaxies, and against the breast of her new mother weeps in awe before losing memory of all that time and all that space; a second later a bomb explodes on a bus in the Holy Land, killing both a scholar of invisibility and a lovesick girl still swooning over the streets of Paris and a man there she'll never see again; then, in the Indian Ocean, a young dolphin cries for his parents but his voice becomes lost in the din of a ship carrying two honeymooners on their way to the Maldives; for hours a cult in Maine performs a strange nude dance in the woods, and despite their leader's pathological claims, the wind is pretty in their hair, which is long on both the men and the women; just now a homeless man on his makeshift bed of blankets and rags beneath a wintry New York night finishes the great American book about the poor man who became rich and nevertheless died for money; and at the same time, in

Phoenix, Arizona, thousands witness a parade of alien lights pass over the desert for the first and last time.

And here a young man and a young woman lie beside each other, mostly skin, all touching, dreaming one dream. I open my eyes; we are them.

THE SEA IS GREAT beyond this boat. We have floated far away from Lyra. I am curled into him. His breath in my ear is slow, deep. How many times will we get to do this, this simplest of things between lovers? Once, never again. He murmurs in his dreams. His hand is cupped over mine, big as a bear's. I open my eyes and turn my neck. It is him. My beauty. His hair is more luscious than in memory, thick and full of curls. His eyes are closed, the lashes over them flutter. He is wearing his brown trousers. His chest is bare. The blue shirt still cast ashore. "Gabriel," I whisper. "Have a look." The night above us is not like nights seen from Earth. Meteorites burn in every direction. There is no atmosphere. "Gabriel," I whisper again as I rise. There are other boats around us, in the thousands, boats of dreaming lovers. The sea is shallow, and just some feet below us, illuminating the sea in sapphire, is his fairy throne. This is the entrance to the land of the dead.

"From here you can almost touch it," Gabriel says, but his voice is no longer in the boat. It arrives upon me like water. "So touch it."

32.

There is no moon tonight, but a beam glows through the fog from a secret satellite. We sit, Simon and I, in our sun-beaten lawn chairs by the ocean on this final evening. At my ankle lies a worn red picnic basket. It must belong to the rest of my life, which has passed behind me. All its faces, all its moments of terror and euphoria, fall back into the tide of memory. Behind us the oaks stretch thick as fur over Lyra, laced in that blue light, stretching from the soil to the sky. It is beginning to burn.

I turn to my husband of all these years. "Simon, do you remember that night, the night Gabriel drowned?" I ask. The sound of my own voice reminds me of whale song, of a woman crying underwater. We are already crossing into different realms, Simon and I.

"Oh, Elle, how many times have we trod this ground? The man was desperate. He drowned himself. It's all very sad." His eyes flutter from drowsiness. Simon will awaken before the dawn, his best suit hanging on the door for the journey, the unanswered letter from Thomas secure in his coat pocket.

Where will he think I am? Saying farewell to the garden, perhaps. It will take him too long to realize I am not anywhere when he runs through the oak, which will appear to him like a dream as the fire gains traction overnight, at last reaching the dunes, an old man, panting there, staring at the sea. His Elle, gone.

Simon will have only enough time before the flames sweep the woods in every direction. He will never have seen a fire so pretty, so blue. And yet Death will not take him. Death will have to claw him out of this life. Simon will run madly west toward the river, toward his world, his Earth.

"Perhaps he wasn't desperate," I say. "Perhaps there is another world waiting for us."

"It's too late, Elle, for all this philosophizing." Simon yawns and rises, preparing to leave.

"Do you think you've been a good person?" I ask. This is the last question I have for my husband. It is simple. After all, we have so little control over anything else.

Simon looks lovingly at me, his eyes that deep Atlantic blue. He is already on the mainland, in Savannah. He has already arrived at tomorrow. "I made my mistakes," he says. "Lord knows. But I know one thing—I always strove to make you happy, Elle. Even when you didn't want it for yourself. And perhaps that has been my downfall."

"Is it really my happiness you wanted, Simon? Or did you want our life together to appear happy? Beautiful as a song you might play on the piano, for some enthralled audience?"

Simon's gaze drifts into the fog. He looks at his watch. "Dear, what's the point in all this? The big sins are behind us now. We are losing paradise. What do you say we call it a night?"

"Very well. I can tell you plainly what would make me truly happy tonight, Simon—a few moments here by the ocean to myself."

"But it's conspiring to rain, Elle."

"Don't fret over me. I even managed not to forget an umbrella." And there one rests on my lap, like a magic trick.

Simon formulates a lecture on the further dangers of my remaining here alone, but I intercept him. "More than anything, Simon, we are alike in exactly one way: we've always wanted things to be beautiful. For me, even if I wasn't always happy, I had this place. You gave me this. All this. The ocean, the woods. I could breathe here. But now that's being taken from us, too. Maybe that's how the end always is. Nothing ends like it does in the movies or a symphony. The end is just loss."

"Why are you talking like this?" Simon asks. "It's not the end of anything. Lyra is ours forever, Elle. We're just leaving it for a little while. We'll be back."

"I know, I know. It's not yet the end," I reply.

"Please don't stay out here too late. Our son will have the car ready for us and waiting at seven."

I must appear suddenly confused. "Raymond," Simon adds for my benefit.

"Yes, our Raymond." I nod confidently.

Simon looks satisfied. "I love these days. The days you come back to us."

He kisses my forehead, and in that last touch it returns—the day Raymond was born, mid-July, wailing upon arrival. I felt just as I had upon giving birth to Zelda, that I had uncovered my treasure, my entire reason for coming to this Earth, and for remaining.

I listen with tenderness as Simon walks the path to the house and disappears beyond the blue gates. "Goodbye," I whisper when his footsteps fade. "Goodbye, Raymond, goodbye, Zelda."

33.

Lyra has receded now. Only the horses remain, dreaming of Earth as it is in heaven. I walk through the fog, the old umbrella raised, toward that steady, strange light that reflects no orb above but a secret constellation in the heart of the ocean itself. I approach the shore. The waves flood over my toes; I become blue, luminescent. The stars have fallen into the sea, a dream become real, when Gabriel appears at last. He reaches for me as I enter the water. I can hear the music now. There has been music all this time. We walk deeper. The rain falls all over us. From the beach I hear a voice call for me, distant and lost beneath the ocean roar. My feet detach from this burning world. I know what I must do. It is time, after all, at last.

Acknowledgments

This novel was blessed with a great many guardian angels to whom I am endlessly grateful. They are Calvert Morgan, who read this first as a diamond in the rough and made it shine; PJ Mark, whose belief, passion, and sincerity are boundless; my grandparents Anne and Seymour, who left New York for a tiny town called Florala at the end of the Great Depression, and lived a life draped in kudzu and Rachmaninoff; Ethel, who lovingly bore witness to Anne at the end; my great-aunt Rhoda, who lit the spark; my mother and father, whose past gave me my future; my brilliant friends (Elena, Danny, Laina, more), who read and commented on this manuscript when it was a scrappy young thing; Autumn, who introduced me to her ocean fairies; Paris, the home of my heart; Cumberland Island, that dream of wild horses, violet sea, haunted trees; New York City, the one and only; and finally, my true treasures—Jake, my once in ten thousand years, and Aurelia, my gem-eyed girl.